THE VIEW FROM THE FISHBOWL

A DISABILITY STORY

By Elizabeth Crounse

Purple Owl Publishing

Newton, MA 02461

TABLE OF CONTENTS

CHAPTER 1

The damn fly sat on the tip of his nose. If he closed his right eye and rolled his left eye to the right, he could just see it. He even saw the compound eye. Or perhaps he imagined it-he had been fascinated by compound eyes since he found a wooden model of one on a third-grade trip to the science museum. He scrunched up his face to the best of his ability, trying to shake the thing off. 'Please not my eyes, please....' He mentally begged the insect. But the ugly thing kept its trudge up the bridge of his nose. He blinked his eyes fast, hoping to frighten it away, but the fly must have known it was safe. He shut his eyes tight as, apparently, that's where the minute monster was headed. JJ's breathing slowed as he sensed the tiny feet patting on the space between the eyes, then a tentative rustle of his eyelashes. The fly stepped onto the shelf of his lashes. He didn't dare open his eyes now. It stepped lightly, leaving God knows what filth behind. He tried again to squint, hoping any movement might shake it loose, but no luck. Tears were welling up in his eyes, which was ridiculous, it was a harmless fly. But he was disgusted and powerless. He tried to think of something else, but the creature had begun to

1

poke around in his lashes to taste the salt- water underneath. The tears were beginning to squeeze out when the door flew open and a booming voice said, "JJ! My man! What we going to do with this fine day?" And the fly was gone.

CHAPTER 2

JJ was hungry by the time breakfast arrived. He had an extensive morning routine, usually taking between 30 to 45 minutes, but when Franklin was on duty that time flew because the guy was incapable of silence. JJ forgot all about the fly as he watched his breakfast being prepared. One egg and 2 slices of turkey bacon, 1 slice of cold whole wheat toast with butter that would never melt. All cut to one-inch pieces, which was what the Occupational Therapist and Speech Therapist had agreed he could tolerate. It was one of the things he first learned to appreciate about Cedar Hills, the group home he lived in. The long-term care facility, aka nursing home, he had resided in previous to this had kept him on a ground diet out of an abundance of caution. It was one of the many indignities JJ had had to endure since his accident.

JJ, as Franklin called him, or sometimes Triple J (his real name was James Joseph Johnson), was feeling much better by the time breakfast ended and morning activities began. Franklin talked constantly, not pausing for a response. "Going to the beach with my lady this weekend Bro, though don't know how much beach

3

we're goin' to see. Got a different kind of surfing in mind, if you know what I mean. Like Beyoncé says, "ride that surfboard" he crooned. JJ had never heard of the song, but then again Franklin was not doing it justice.

JJ did know what Franklin was talking about, though Maria and Supervisor would be shocked to find this out. He had been a guy who had run with a crew. He knew some things, had done some things, was a far cry from a choir boy. He had a reputation, prior to the accident, as a bit of a player. He was a better man now; he had become a more patient, thoughtful person than his 17- year old self.

The women in the house viewed him as an innocent, naïve boy, a perennial child, because of his disability, and his level of dependence would do nothing to discourage that characterization. But he had lived a full life till the accident, and his life since required the resilience and maturity to navigate which was decidedly not childlike. Sometimes he felt emasculated, but he would not deny that he sometimes enjoyed the maternal attention that he received from the women of the house, and on a bad day being kissed on the forehead or embraced gave him the sense of being cared for that he hadn't experienced since his mother died. He guessed everyone needed a Mom, but everyone needed a Franklin too.

The schedule called for nature documentaries, but JJ thought he might just close his eyes for a while. Surprisingly, he had very little interest in the migration habits of birds. His eyes took in the room in front of him and saw most of his 11 housemates nodding off. A couple of lucky ones had program outside of the house or were on outings, the rest of them had habilitation activities at the house. Generally, that was ok, but on rainy days, when Nature Videos was on the calendar, JJ knew he was going to have an extra nap.

Staff gathered around the dining room table with mugs of coffee, but Franklin always sat next to JJ and tried to keep him entertained. If he joined the other staff for coffee or gossip, he brought JJ with him. The others who lived in the house shared staff with two or three peers, but Franklin had JJ, and on short days, only one other individual, usually JJ's roommate Wayne. This might be because JJ's physical needs were greater, or because he emotionally needed a great deal of interaction or he became despondent. When Franklin first worked with JJ the chemistry was so obvious that he became his regular staff. On Franklin's days off he would typically have Julie, who was a sweetheart. She was going to nursing school part-time, so she was always very good about his care.

"The Robin, sometimes called Robin Red Breast, is among the first of the northeast's birds to arrive in the spring..." As JJ's head began to drop, Derrick came over and in a low voice, said "Hey, Franklin, I got a bootleg of Crusher."

Franklin had just come back with JJ's 10 o'clock snack. "How the hell did you get that?" Franklin seemed impressed.

"I got my ways. Told you the site, I don't know why you couldn't get in."

Derrick was JJ's 2nd favorite male staff. Supervisor would not like how Derrick talked to JJ either. He was a 20-year-old who had come to the agency when he was 18, right out of high school. He swore this was not his career, he intended to move on when he figured out what he wanted to do with his life, but he seemed pretty comfortable to JJ. He doubted Derrick would be leaving any time soon. "Who've you got today?" Franklin asked as he scanned the room. "I'm a float. Let me do the kitchen and I can take a break." Derrick hurried off to the kitchen where he started on the dishes and kitchen clean up while Franklin gave JJ his 4-ounce cup of pudding. "Ok JJ, let's lose this bird crap, ok? Unless you're interested in it. Your choice. But I think you'll like Crusher 11. Crusher I was amazing. So, we good?" JJ gave the slight twitch of his lip in consent.

In a loud voice, Franklin said "You ok JJ? You look a little pale." And to the nurse who was walking past, "I think I'm going to put him down a little early, he didn't eat that much and he's looking a little off." The nurse was not persuaded by his apparent concern, but she was busy and not inclined to argue. "Ok but have him up for lunch. If he doesn't perk up, I'll have a look later."

Back in his room Franklin put JJ to bed using the lift. Ordinarily this would have pissed JJ off: he spent way too much time in bed. But he was always down for one of Franklin's schemes. While the motor of the lift groaned with his weight, Franklin leaned close and gave him the plot to Crusher I. Lots of action, some chase scenes, some violence, some sex, and in the end the hero loses the girl. Franklin guessed Crusher II was probably more of the same. It wasn't coming out till next week, but Derrick knew some dark website where you could buy bootleg. "You see

Wolverine when it came out? You would have been 16 or 17, right? Yeah, you probably seen it. It's kind of like Wolverine." Franklin always provided both sides of the conversation.

A minute later Derrick came in with JJ's roommate Wayne. This annoyed JJ, who thought it was just going to be the three of them, but then he realized Derrick would need a reason to be in the room, and Wayne was his cover. JJ had nothing against Wayne, but he and JJ were not friends. He didn't seem to be very "with it", though JJ realized the same could be said of him if one judged by appearances alone.

While Derrick plugged a utility cable into his phone and Wayne's TV and turned it, so they were all able to see, Franklin tuned to a music channel on JJ's TV and set the volume very low. If Supervisor came in the room, she would find them all glued to the TV music channel and enjoying classical jazz, and Wayne's TV would be off. This was not the first time these two had done this. Franklin turned the lights off, and he and Derrick each took a seat between the beds.

Crusher turned out to be everything the hype said it would be. The fight scenes were amazing. The sex scenes were hot. Derrick and Franklin sat at the edge of their seats, watching, but also listening for anyone who may come in, and prepared to kill Wayne's TV if necessary. Every five minutes Derrick would go check on one of their other charges, then come back.

After close to an hour, Derrick heard Supervisor coming and cut the video, whispering to JJ, "we'll finish it later." Wayne was

sound asleep by then, and Derrick stepped out of the room inno-
cently just as Supervisor entered to find Franklin dutifully discon-
necting JJ's urine bag. He looked up and said "just going to empty
this and then I'm going to see to Michael. I hated to leave him
because I know he doesn't like being alone in here." He somberly
tilted his head towards JJ. Supervisor looked suspicious but let it
go. JJ had closed his eyes when she entered and appeared to be
taking a nap. Franklin emptied the bag and reattached it, and as
he followed Supervisor out, he turned to JJ and winked.

JJ closed his eyes contentedly as he actually did drift off to
sleep. When he woke 45 minutes later, he sensed, rather than
heard, someone in the room. Wayne's brother was there. JJ did
not like the guy and didn't trust him at all, though he couldn't
have told you why. The brother's name was Gary. He was some
kind of lawyer, and he visited every day, bringing Wayne a chocolate shake. JJ would have killed for a chocolate shake. The guy
smelled of Versace Cologne. JJ only knew that because Valerie, a
new young staff, spent an hour at the perfume counter at Macy's
until she finally identified the scent. His suits were Italian, she
was pretty sure. He drove a Mercedes convertible, and Valerie
wasn't the only woman in the house who hoped for a ride in it.
JJ thought it was disgusting! She couldn't be more than 24, and
Gary must have been over 40. They were all so impressed that
this good looking, rich, busy man would come almost every lunch
hour to spend fifteen minutes with his brother. Such devotion!

He had never been involved with Wayne in the past, including
most of the last two years that Wayne had lived at the house.
Wayne had a Mom who adored him and came most days to bring

him some treat or cut his nails or just stroke his hand. She had been sick for almost a year, and her visits became less frequent till they stopped completely. Suddenly four months ago Gary had begun to take an interest, allegedly at his mother's request. He was very ostentatious about it. On his way into the room, JJ could hear him flirting with the staff: "How did my brother luck out and get staff like you girls? I hope he knows how lucky he is." Some of the women staff were absolutely smitten with him.

JJ knew the truth. When he came into the room, he never so much as said hi to Wayne, unless a staff was around to hear him. Usually JJ could not see him, unless Gary wandered to his side of the room when he was doing his email or talking on the phone. But JJ could hear, and no kind words were ever spoken. If a staff did enter the room, the guy would rush to the bedside and pat Wayne's hand, gushing "How's my big brother today?" The charade ended when they were alone. Why he came was a mystery. JJ sensed he was doing something, but whatever that something was, was happening out of JJ's field of vision.

After lunch (egg salad and celery, strawberries for desert), JJ was taken back to his room to "freshen up". Derrick was already there with Wayne, who had been changed and returned to his bed. He was very weak lately and his medical staff had ordered more rest and extra blood work. Derrick had the utility cord plugged in to Wayne's TV and as soon as JJ was cleaned up, they finished the movie, though this time JJ was able to sit up. JJ suffered from GERD (Gastroesophageal Reflux Disorder) which required him to stay upright for a half hour after meals. He felt more like one of the guys when he sat with them, instead of lying in bed.

'The movie rocked! Awesome! Going to be a classic' Franklin declared. And to think he saw it before anyone else! Good to have friends.

Franklin took him back to the Dining Room for a 2:00 snack, an inedible cookie and some sugar free Kool-Aid type drink. As Franklin gave JJ the food he rambled on about the movie to JJ, reviewing every scene, asking and answering his own questions. Then back for afternoon repositioning. As he left, Franklin raised JJ's hand for their usual fist bump and said, "Good times Bro, Good times."

JJ fell asleep happy.

CHAPTER 3

When he woke up JJ checked the clock. Already 4:00. He must have slept for an hour. It had been a satisfying day, and this evening, Maria was his staff. She promised him Peanut Butter Blossom cookies tonight. She was assigned to cook dinner, and tonight the menu called for meatloaf, which she knew he loved. She would bring him to the kitchen with her while she cooked, just like his mom used to when she was alive. He learned a fair amount about cooking from his Mom, and when she died during his freshman year of high school, he largely took on most of the meal prep for himself and his dad. He would rush home from school, whip up some hamburgers or meatloaf, baked or mashed potatoes, warm up a can of vegetables. But this finally ended when he realized the only meal his Dad wanted came in a six-pack. After that JJ ate mostly frozen pizza and fast food.

He shut his eyes: he knew he had another 15 minutes to kill and thinking of his mother started him on a trip into his younger years, which was rare-he tried not to dwell in the past. Sometimes he still found it amazing how quickly his life had changed direction, not once, but twice.

JJ spent his teenage years largely unsupervised. Dad took his wife's death from cancer badly and withdrew into the bottle, coming out of his stupor only occasionally to see if JJ was still okay. JJ and his Dad were very close until then-best buds, really. His Dad taught him woodworking, took him fishing, attended all his track meets, ran interference with his Mom. After his Mom's death, it was like he lost both parents.

Friends filled the gap, and JJ wasn't the best at choosing the right friends. But he did okay, for the most part, and while not working to potential at school, he was a solid B. That was far better than the guys he hung with and good enough to get him into a state college. He ran with a crowd that drank and smoked and partied, and he would join them, but still manage to get homework done and get to school most days. If not for the accident, he would have his four-year degree in Geology right now, probably be married and with a kid or two. Instead, here he was, lying in bed waiting for staff to help him up, wash his backside, empty his urine bag, and wipe away the drool. He was totally dependent on the kindness of strangers, so to speak.

Maria was by far his favorite staff. While Franklin and Derrick made him feel young and hip and masculine, Maria made him feel loved. She fussed over him like he was her son, though he was only 5 or 6 years younger than her. His life got better the day he met her, and he sometimes thought if there was, in fact, a heaven, and if his mother was looking down on him, she would have sent Maria.

At 4:20 JJ got a bit nervous. Maria was the most reliable staff in the house. She worked her schedule like clockwork, in by 3:55, reading report and checking updates till 4:10, throwing open the door with a cheery "How's my favorite guy?" at 4:15. For her, this was late. At 4:25 he knew something was wrong. Then his worst fears were confirmed: Jason's voice was loud and angry in the hall: "No problem, I'll work another friggin' 8 hours. I'll just tell my girlfriend to throw out dinner cause I'm MANDATED. No problem. I hate this f-in place." The door flew open and he stormed in with Supervisor behind him, trying to soothe him. He shut the door in her face and dropped the bed rail aggressively without even glancing at JJ. He emptied the urine bag, checked JJ's incontinence brief (or as JJ thought of it, diaper) and then unceremoniously strapped the lift around him and deposited him into the chair. 'Damn, Jason, don't forget my orthotic.' JJ thought to himself. He breathed a sigh of relief when Jason glanced around and yanked the molded plastic body support off the top of the wardrobe. He opened the plastic jacket and tried to wrap it around JJ's trunk, but unsuccessfully since he forgot to take off the seat belt. Jason tried twice, then muttered "fuck it" and tossed it aside.

Jason wheeled JJ to the dining room and put his phone to his ear, where he spent the next hour complaining to his girlfriend that his job sucked. JJ glared at him, but Jason never noticed. He smelled of old beer and gas station pizza. Proud of his ignorance, wearing his flannel shirt and an old hat with some tool company's logo, he strutted around almost daring people to brawl. He thought the work was beneath him and told everyone who would listen he was just waiting to get a job in construction. Many staff hoped he would get a job in construction, too. His swagger was not founded on any observable positive attributes as far as JJ

13

could see. But somehow, even though he was disliked by most of the staff and certainly Supervisor, Jason managed to stay this side of abusive and lingered on month after month. JJ knew he would be put to bed much earlier than he was supposed to by this jerk, but he didn't care. The less time spent in Jason's presence the better.

Ten minutes later JJ's face was pressed against the tray of his wheelchair and a pool of saliva his took shape under his mouth. He had tried to remain upright but only managed about five minutes before the weight of his head became more than his neck could sustain, and gravity pulled it down, pulling his upper body with it till he was faceplanted on his tray. He listened, hoping someone other than the psychopath who was assigned to him would take notice and save him. He was ok for now, but he knew soon his position would begin to restrict his breathing and he would be in trouble.

The orthotic jacket was made of a stiff plastic, and was molded to his body, from his clavicle to his hips. It took the burden of supporting his trunk so that he could use the little muscle tone he had left to support his head in an upright position. With the jacket and a seat belt, he could be supported in a 90- degree posture during meals. Without the jacket he was a helpless puddle, and his lungs would not expand to their maximum capacity, and certainly his esophagus would be constricted. He needed his orthosis, and all the staff knew it.

Jason often took short cuts when he was assigned to individuals with more complex needs, so he was generally given people who were less disabled. JJ thought staffing must be bad tonight for Supervisor to give him to Jason. It had nothing to do with Jason disliking JJ, it was more that he didn't think of him as a human being. He was an assignment, a chore to carry out. JJ despised Jason but he took some comfort in knowing Maria would be furious to find out Jason had been his staff. She would be sputtering about it all tomorrow evening.

Fifteen minutes had gone by and JJ started to worry. No one had noticed his predicament, and he could tell his breathing was becoming shallow. His face was wet from the drool puddling beneath him. He breathed through his nose so as not to inhale the saliva. Shit was getting real, as Franklin would say.

These kinds of episodes sometimes brought back the ghosts of the past, when he was not a helpless victim of a bar room bully like Jason. At 17 JJ was not that different from Jason, minus the cruel streak and with a more hopeful future. His fortunes changed abruptly one day and while JJ couldn't remember the accident and the immediate aftermath, he remembered vividly what came before.

JJ learned to drive with his older buddies, which wasn't legal, but neither would driving with his inebriated father have been. He decided he was ready for his driving test when the local greens keeper offered him a part time job, with the condition he get a license. The night before the test, he suddenly lost his confidence and thought he had better practice some of his turns. He asked his Dad to take him out, but unfortunately, his Dad was finishing his first six pack, so JJ went out alone. He lost control on some pavement, hit a tree, and after numerous days in the hospital, many surgeries and failed attempts at rehab, it was finally clear that the paralysis was permanent. A short, life changing story. Most would say a tragic story.

JJ's reminiscing ended when he realized he was becoming light-headed. His chest was compressed against the wheelchair tray, and he was afraid he was going to pass out. Just as he began to panic Jason clicked off his phone and tossed it on the table. He shoved JJ's body back in his seat and dropped the back of his chair by 20 degrees so that his head was accessible for feeding, then went to make up JJ's plate. JJ was immediately relieved to draw a deep breath, then realized he was about to be fed in a position that almost guaranteed choking.

The meal was a disaster. The menu called for meatloaf, which JJ assumed must be what this mush of ground tasteless meat was supposed to be. Jason couldn't be bothered with adding condiments like ketchup. He continued to rail against the management throughout the meal to whoever was on the opposite end of the table, but not surprisingly after the first person was finished, subsequent diners were assisted at other tables.

Jason brought the fork to JJ's mouth without so much as eye contact to see if it was hitting the mark. At one point, Valerie, who was sitting across from them, cried out "careful!" just in time to prevent JJ from being stabbed in the eye. She seemed troubled by what she was seeing, but having only been there a few months, was hesitant to correct senior staff. She ventured at one point a meek observation,

"He looks like he may not be in his chair right" but retreated when Jason retorted,

"Been here a few weeks and you think you know more than I do?"

She finished the meal and gave Miriam dessert at a different table.

JJ did the best he could to protect himself. On the occasions the food actually stayed on the fork and made it to his mouth, he pushed it back out with his tongue. Jason didn't notice or didn't care. His eyes were on his phone, reading and texting. The peas rolled off the fork anyway. JJ had some luck managing the potatoes with his tongue and swallowed them without choking.

As JJ grew anxious and angry, he did what he always did when frustration overwhelmed him: he tried to imagine scenarios in which his tribulations would be avenged. He envisioned Maria coming in tomorrow, trying to make up to him for having had to call in. He would avoid eye contact with her for most of the shift as punishment. He would look as sad as possible, and not eat well (unless it was a favorite dish), would not let her off easy. Not after the evening he had with psycho Jason. Of course, he knew what he was dealing with was not directly her fault, but there was no denying her calling in had set the disaster in motion.

And for Jason, well, JJ could be borderline cruel. He thought that most likely Jason would speed home, and on the way, hopefully be stopped by the police. He would run his mouth and they would rough him up a bit before taking him off to jail. The guy didn't have any money, JJ was fairly sure, so he figured when he called his girlfriend, she would dump him right after refusing to bail him out. The agency would get wind of it and would fire him, and he wouldn't be able to make his beloved truck's payments, and it would be repossessed....

JJ's hateful musings ended when suddenly a piece of meatloaf escaped his notice and slid down his throat before his tongue could intervene. He started choking. Honest to God choking! Jason, who was now watching sports news, kept obliviously shoveling food in or in the vicinity of his mouth. JJ's eyes grew wide and his whole immobile body tensed as he tried to dislodge the meat from his trachea. He was about to pass out when he heard Supervisor shriek "He's choking!" as she exited her office and flew across the room. Jason paled, pulled JJ's wheelchair tray off and unfastened the seat belt. Supervisor pulled him forward and did the Heimlich. After three attempts, a hunk of meat flew out of JJ's mouth and hit Jason in the face, which, in spite of JJ's distress, gave him some satisfaction.

The next fifteen minutes were almost worth the terror he'd experienced. Supervisor hugged JJ's head to her ample breasts and kept repeating "are you alright sweetheart?" JJ smirked and glared at Jason straight in the eye until Jason sheepishly turned away. When she finished comforting him, she stood up and shrieked "where is his jacket?"

Jason stammered, "Does he have one? I hardly ever work with him. I didn't know..." She glared at him and he scurried away to retrieve it.

The supervisor put the orthotic jacket on, chastising Jason as she did so. Why was his chair reclined? Why was his meatloaf not cut up smaller? Why is the bulk of the meal on the floor and his shirt? Jason stopped trying to answer and just took the tongue lashing. He had no excuse.

Supervisor got JJ a drink and called the nurse who directed that he be taken to the emergency room to be cleared.

Sweet! Any chance to take a trip was a good time. And when he learned that Jason was being sent home pending an investigation and Franklin had agreed to come in to take him, he felt like he hit the lottery. Maybe he'd even let Maria off the hook for putting this whole event into play by calling out-she will be so upset that this happened, she will have suffered enough.

CHAPTER 4

Getting up after his late night at the Emergency Room was tough. He lay in bed after being given his meds, thankful that Julie was not a morning person either and was giving him a minute before making him move. He lay with his eyes shut, inhaling the clean smell of the room. Gina must have been on last night, though he hadn't seen her. When she worked his whole world shone and smelled like lilacs, even though he never woke up and saw her cleaning. She was a quiet, sweet woman, and while she rarely spoke, she smiled at him whenever their eyes met. She had a nice smile.

The sheets were crisp and felt great under his cheek. The kitchen smelled of coffee brewing and pancakes cooking and maple syrup. He kept his eyes shut but could feel the warm sunlight on his face from the window next to the bed. The window was open, and he could hear the birds, probably having breakfast at the feeder, chatting to each other. The air had that heavy, sultry smell that follows a night of rain. It had been a warmer than usual April.

His mind was replaying last night: Franklin had been funny, flirting with the nurses, who in turn flirted with JJ. While they were waiting, Franklin let him watch the whole of Crusher 1 on the phone, even though it must have killed his arm to hold the phone up for almost 2 hours. After three hours and a few breathing treatments, JJ was sent home with a clean bill of health. He hoped no one told Jason he was ok: let him worry about his job a little longer.

Supervisor had stayed late so she could be there when he got back. She let Franklin go home and spent the last hour covering herself until the night shift came in. She let JJ stay up a little while before getting him to bed to make sure he was alright, getting him a piece of pie for desert and a cup of tea, and chatting to him about what she was going to do to make sure what happened tonight never happened again. She seemed to take the incident very personally.

JJ smiled to himself. This morning his near miss seemed like a good story, but last night's incident, he realized, could have ended his life. Supervisor seemed to realize how close he had come. She really was very conscientious and seemed to feel responsible for having assigned Jason to work with him. She generally made sure Wayne, JJ and others with complex needs got her best staff, but last night was a tough night for staffing, and Jason, she thought, was the best she could do for him. Clearly it was a mistake.

Supervisor had been there since JJ had arrived at the house, and while he initially had been very reserved with her, he had come to like her and appreciate how hard she worked. He never actually thought of her by name, which was Mona. He thought of her as Supervisor. Where he had come from, staff came and went constantly, and he had learned to think of them as positions, not as people. He would always have a supervisor, but they may not always be named Mona.

He had experienced some close calls early on after his accident, but not recently. Truthfully, it brought home how utterly defenseless he was, and that always brought him down for a while.

His mind drifted back to waking up at the hospital after the accident, the first time he had experienced the loss of control that he had lived with ever since. There had been concern about the brain trauma in addition to the spinal injury initially. He would wake and stare at individuals in his room, but no names or labels would come to mind. They had begun to prepare his father for the fact that he may never have the ability to communicate, think, feel emotions etc. But after a while his brain began to function, and the figures floating in and out of his sight would be named: doctors, nurses, his father, his English teacher, the neighbor Mr. Jenson for whom JJ sometimes mowed the lawn. Then the questions: 'what had happened? Where am I? Why can't I feel my legs, or move my arms, etc.?' And finally, the emotions flooded in, as answers to those questions came with little snippets of overheard conversations..."not going to be able to walk again...paralyzed...spinal injury...voice box injury".

In the final analysis, JJ's mind functioned just fine, other than some lost memory from the accident and shortly afterwards, but there was really no way for him to convey that. Only those that were very close to him perceived his level of understanding, and he was pretty sure they underestimated it greatly.

He protected his mental skills aggressively; he read anything that was in eyeshot, did computations in his head, listened intently to news and documentaries so he could stay informed and feel relevant. He would quiz himself about science, history, everything he had ever learned, trying to hold on to every morsel of what he knew, trying to hold on to James Joseph Johnson.

His body had not fared so well. His spinal injury was very high, and he had literally no function in his legs or trunk muscles. His right arm hung useless, and at first glance one might think the same was true of his left, but he actually could move his left arm and fingers. With a great deal of effort, he could push his arm an inch or two either way, using his fingers to crawl one way or another, dragging the arm with them. He practiced moving his arm two inches like it was an Olympic Sport. He would walk his fingers a couple of inches till he felt the bedrail, hook them, and pull with all his might. His body would rotate to the left, an inch, an inch and a half? He didn't know if it would ever become useful, but he wasn't about to give up any ground at this point. For him moving his arm at his side two inches *was* an Olympic event.

Thank God his swallowing mechanism was intact. He lived in fear of being put on a ground or soft diet: for a meat and potatoes guy like him, that would have killed him. His sense of smell was good, and he learned to love the variety of odors that stimulated, or assaulted, his nose. He could see well but only directly in front of him. He could not turn his head. He could hold his head up for short periods of time, but it would topple over after a few minutes without the extra support of the orthosis.

So, this was him, the new him, and he had learned first to accept, then to love, himself with the help of Maria and others who had come before her.

Julie finally came in and said "Time's Up! If we don't get you out there now you will miss out on breakfast!" He got to the dining room just in time and realized just how famished he was. He had a leisurely breakfast, just he and Julie in the room, and she sat and had a cup of coffee with him before taking him out for a short walk. Julie was also assigned to Wayne, so she was splitting her time between them, which gave JJ some time to relax and reflect on the previous day's events, and to wonder about Maria.

JJ was back in bed for his hour of re-positioning just before lunch. The nurse was concerned about a reddened area on his butt, so she ordered him positioned on his left side with pillows. That gave him a whole different view of his room. He was anxious to be able to see what Wayne's brother was up to and was determined to stay awake to watch.

Gary arrived at the usual time and walked into the room, and since no staff was there, he ignored Wayne. Once the door was closed, he walked to Wayne's bed without so much a glance at his brother. His phone was buzzing with messages, and Gary was annoyed by whatever he was reading. He finally punched some numbers in the phone and spoke to the sender,

"Ok, what part of this plan don't you understand?"

He listened impatiently then cut the speaker off.

"Ok I'm going to tell you this one more time. She's 92 years old. She doesn't know you or me from Pope Francis, and we're her sons. She is not suffering by staying home. I know she burns out her aides but replace them! Raise their salaries if you need to! If she goes to a home the state will take most of her money. She wouldn't want that! Six months ago, they said the cancer would take her in six months. We don't have that much longer. Keep the aides. I'm doing my bit, you do yours."

And with that he hung up the phone, and in doing so glanced at JJ. Something in JJ's expression seemed to catch him by surprise. He didn't say anything but looked at JJ for a long minute. Having decided that JJ was not a threat, Gary walked over to the bedside table where he had deposited the milkshake, took the top off and reached into his pocket. Whatever he did next JJ couldn't see, but he suspected that Gary put something in the shake before putting the top back on. There was a slight medicinal smell.

Gary stuffed a straw into the lid and held it to Wayne's mouth. Wayne took a couple of sips then seemed to lose interest. The brother impatiently ripped the top off, opened Wayne's mouth and poured in the contents. Wayne sputtered and swallowed as fast he could. JJ felt for him, knowing what it felt like to choke the night before, and wanted to make it stop, but other than glaring at Gary JJ was helpless.

Julie came in to get JJ but stopped when she saw JJ's face. She followed his gaze and saw the shake all over Wayne's face and oozing out of his mouth while he struggled to swallow. "Oh Dear!" she gasped.

Jerry/Gary quickly hid the cup and said, "He must be really thirsty; I couldn't slow him down." He looked a bit sheepish as Julie took charge, sitting Wayne up higher and wiping his face with some tissue.

"You ok sweetheart?" she asked Wayne. "Mr. Whitestone," she said sternly. "Have you been shown how Wayne drinks? He really needs a straw."

Mr. Whitestone was syrupy sweet:

"First, call me Gary. And yes, I have been shown, but today he didn't seem to be able to draw it up, so I tried the cup. I won't do that again! Thanks for your help! Wayne is lucky you were here."

He left with a wave to his brother for Julie's sake. Wayne looked shook up but gradually calmed down as Julie cleaned him up and soothed him. JJ really felt bad for the guy. So Scary Gary was a creep, just as JJ suspected. Outside of that JJ did not really understand what was going on, but he was determined to pay attention to his visits from now on.

CHAPTER 5

At 4:15 it was clear that the world had righted itself when Maria threw open the door with a cheery "How's my favorite guy?" JJ immediately forgot about his plan for vengeance and curled his lip in his best smile and made the best eye contact he could to show her how relieved he was to see her. Maria busied herself checking him out, taking care of his needs, all the while expressing her utter disgust that Mona had assigned Jason, of all people, that good for nothing Jason, to take care of her guy. She was properly indignant, and JJ just basked in the glow of self-righteousness as he listened to her.

But as she leaned over him to get him ready for the lift, he thought he saw a hint of sadness, or worry, in her eyes. Her voice was cheery and affectionate, but there was something below the surface. And he was pretty sure he saw a small bruise on her cheek.

Suddenly he felt ashamed that he never thought of her as a person with her own life. He knew she had a boyfriend, no children, and had lost both her parents in the past. She told him once that was why she was there for him-she knew what it was like to have no one looking out for you. He always assumed she was happy because that was all she let him see. But today she looked troubled, and he wished he could be there for her the way she was there for him.

Maria brought him to the kitchen while she cooked. Tonight's meal was chicken with mashed potatoes and steamed carrots. He sat next to her while she sprinkled and peeled and mashed and she chattered about the Spanish food she made at home and her mother's cooking. She let him smell the seasoning as she prepared the chicken, let him taste the potatoes before they were put in a serving dish, and gave him a piece of raw carrot before steaming them. Being in the kitchen with Maria reminded him so much of him and his Mom when he was young, tears welled up in his eyes. He really loved this woman.

Dinner was delicious. While Maria and the other staff swapped stories, everyone laughed throughout the meal. Wayne sat nearby and seemed to actually make eye contact with JJ a couple of times. JJ thought maybe he had judged him too quickly.

The rest of the evening was pleasant but uneventful. Back in his room he tried very hard to smile his thanks to Maria as she got him ready for bed. The door opened and Julie's head popped in.

"Maria, Brad's on the phone. Do you want to take it?"

Maria's face froze. In an even tone she replied: "Tell him I'm very busy and I'll call him tomorrow."

As she finished up, she was very quiet. She was out of JJ's field of vision, but when she bent down to kiss his forehead good night a teardrop fell on his cheek, betraying the lie in her cheery "good night".

CHAPTER 6

JJ was awake but kept his eyes closed. He guessed it was around seven o'clock. He had learned that they would not get him up as early if they believed he was still asleep, and this was a favorite time of the day. He lay there trying to figure out what the day was likely to hold for him. From the kitchen he could smell bacon, so breakfast was probably bacon and eggs. Lunch would be a surprise. Dinner, however, if Maria was right, would be pork chops, and those were one of his favorite foods. If the menu was the same as last month, there would be rice pilaf, another favorite, and if he remembered correctly, Brussel sprouts, which he could take or leave.

He tried to remember how many outings he had this month. He was entitled to two. It was April 21st and he could only remember having had one: a trip to the Aquarium. Maria took him and he really enjoyed it. They lingered in front of massive tanks and watched the myriad of colors. When he left, he thought it would be nice to have a fish tank in his room. Miriam had one in her room, so they must be allowed. Maybe Maria would figure it out. Maria seemed to be able to read his mind sometimes.

He hoped that today would not be his outing day, because as much as he liked Julie, he always had the most fun with Franklin, so he was hoping to hold off for tomorrow when Franklin was back on shift.

In 15 days, it would be his 27th birthday: May 6th. Not that it would be a big deal. He would receive a card from his peers, probably one from Maria. A gift bought from his own funds, which he found amusing, and a piece of cake with a candle in it. The whole group would sing to him, but only he would have cake. They used to all share in a birthday cake, but the dietician had decided that if they had a cake for everyone's birthday some people could be getting too many calories, so now you had to eat yours in front of 11 other envious faces.

He wondered if his old man would think about him on his birthday. He used to make an appearance on or around the day. He sometimes had a gift, or a card with a few dollars in it, but he had long ago lost any connection with the son who had once been the light of his life, so JJ often felt the cards were about as meaningful as the Christmas cards they used to get from the bank. A few times over the years JJ would have sworn he saw him, on the street watching as he was lowered on the van lift and brought into the house. If it had been him, he never came in. JJ didn't want to see him anyway. He was part of his old life and he would add nothing to his present.

JJ stopped his musings when he heard Maria's name. Julie entered his room with her phone to her ear, and JJ kept his eyes shut, eavesdropping on what was obviously a phone conversation.

"Maria, I don't mean to interfere, but you have been telling me for months that he is getting more abusive. Then he brings you flowers or takes you to dinner and all is forgiven. It's classic! It's not going to stop. I worry that he will really hurt you. I know it's a hard decision, but you made it-now stick to it! How long can you stay at your sister's apartment? Well, when does she get back from vacation? Does he know where you're staying? Well be careful and call if you need anything. Love you too!

JJ opened his eyes as Julie ended the call and she greeted him with a smile, oblivious to the worry she had just planted in JJ's mind. He had no idea Maria was in an abusive relationship. He was glad Julie had her back; hopefully Maria would listen to her!

Julie was young, just like most of the other staff. She was almost finished with her nursing studies and JJ was going to be sad when she left to find another job. There was only one part time nurse and Cedar Hills and the position was just filled. Julie had gotten married a few months ago, then went on a honeymoon to Bermuda. She had brought back shell wind chimes for each of the home's residents, and they would softly click in the windows when they aired the rooms out.

Julie hurried JJ through his morning routine and out to breakfast, where he was the last one to eat.

Afterwards, the day was nice, so Julie took him for a walk around the block. She paused to let him see a neighbor's dog, holding it up into his line of sight after getting permission from the owner. The dog unexpectedly lurched forward and licked JJ's face with a big slurp which they all found very funny.

JJ loved dogs. He wondered how his dog Scout had fared after the accident. The big goofy golden retriever had been a puppy when he got him for his 13th birthday. He missed Scout more than he missed his Dad. It was Scout who never failed to greet him when he got home when his Dad was passed out in bed. It was Scout who would not leave his side when the tears flowed late at night after his Mom died. JJ was glad that when Scout had bounded after him that terrible night hoping for a ride, he had sent him back to the house. JJ never saw him again after the accident and had no way of asking about him. He would have liked to say goodbye. Hopefully his dad had found him a good home. God knows his Dad couldn't take care of him.

At lunch Supervisor came to the table and excitedly told him she had shopped for his summer clothes. She pulled them out one by one. Polo shirts: Yellow, Blue, and Green. Plaid shorts in the same colors, the type worn largely by middle aged golfers. A pair of blue jean shorts that she thought looked very "hip" (did they still make them? Or was this left over stock from the 80's?) She was not very perceptive of JJ's expressions, so he was glad that she seemed to take his blank affect as approval. Franklin would try them on and make sure they fit. The last time she shopped for him, Franklin convinced her what she bought was the wrong size and returned everything, bringing home replacements much more like JJ would have bought for himself. He hoped Franklin pulled that off again.

CHAPTER 7

The door creaked just as JJ woke up from his afternoon nap. As he opened his eyes, he saw the demonic brother of his roommate leaving. Damn! He must have dozed off. JJ had wanted to keep an eye on him. Figuratively speaking, of course, because today JJ was positioned on his back so he would not have seen much of him anyway. But he could have listened. He vowed to stay awake tomorrow till after the creep left.

Alternate positioning used to be an hour long. It had somehow evolved into an hour and a half to 2 hours long. JJ would hang out in the dining room for a half hour while lunch was cleaned up because of his GERD. He would be taken back to the room, and "freshened up" as Supervisor euphemistically referred to emptying his urine bag, changing a soiled diaper if necessary, and washing his face. Then he would be prepared for the lift. He sat on a mesh cloth sling that was always in his chair. Hooks would be attached to its metal rings and he would be lifted into the air. He kind of enjoyed this feeling of suspension, swinging weightless in the air. The lift would then be lowered until he was laid flat on the bed. He would then be rolled to one side, then the

other, and the sling would be removed. It was quite the procedure, and sometimes in a hurry a noncompliant staff would just
lift his 95 pounds of dead weight and dump him in the bed. Only
a few were strong enough to do so, and if they got caught, they
could be fired. The agency had a strict no lift policy.

He watched the tv for a while, which was tuned to a dull
cooking show. They were making some kind of green salad. All
green salad looked alike to JJ, and pretty much tasted alike too.
He was a meat and potatoes man. If they didn't keep spooning
them into his mouth, he probably wouldn't eat vegetables at all.

He lazed away the next hour and half, in and out of slumber
and alternately watching the tv, which was now showing a much
more interesting chocolate candy making episode "just in time for
Mother's Day".

He remembered one Saturday in May when he was around 12
or 13. His dad had given his mother a gift of having her nails
done and a massage and had sent her off so that he and JJ could
make a cake for her. JJ had made cakes in the past with his Mom,
but this was a first time with his Dad. While they mixed and
spooned and frosted, his Dad told him stories about his Mom and
how they had met. When he found out she was pregnant with JJ
he was more scared than excited, till he saw how she transformed
into a confident and devoted mother and how beautiful mother-
hood made her. He asked JJ what he thought about someday having a new brother or sister. It was the day JJ saw just how much
his Dad loved his Mom and it was the only tender memory left of
his Dad that he still allowed himself to keep.

The next day was Mother's Day, and while eating cake, he was given a gift. It was a baseball cap that said, "Big Brother". They talked about a new baby excitedly. He would have to share his room till they got a bigger place. JJ was going to have to help out more as Mom got further along. They tossed around names for if it was a boy and if it was a girl. They laughed at how big Mom's belly had gotten with JJ and Dad mimicked her waddling like a duck around the kitchen. By far one of the happiest days of his life.

Then two weeks later, her visit to the Obstetrician. It wasn't pregnancy. It was Ovarian Cancer. Ten months later she was gone. Another short, tragic story.

CHAPTER 8

Maria had called in again, but this time JJ was forewarned. He heard Julie talking to Joe in the hall a little after 4:00. JJ knew something was up as soon as he heard Joe's voice, because Joe was a night shaft staff who would generally not be there until 11, so he must have been asked to do overtime.

JJ was right- Joe was replacing Maria. Now JJ was very worried about Maria-this was totally out of character.

JJ revised his expectations for the evening. It should be fine, but everything would take longer because Joe was much slower than other staff. A nice guy, though. By the time he cleaned JJ up and got him in the wheelchair it was nearly time for dinner. He wasn't assigned to anyone else, both as consideration for his double shift and because Supervisor knew it would be all he could do to handle JJ. He just kind of ambled around, his 260-pound body stressing his heart and his knees. He was, maybe 60ish, kind and comfortable and he and JJ generally got along just fine.

From the kitchen JJ smelled what he thought was probably the pork chops he was expecting. After dinner there would be an hour of TV time, and with the crew on tonight, it would probably be set to Jeopardy, which JJ really liked. He was particularly looking forward to it tonight because the all-time champion was about to break another record. It had become pretty exciting, and even Supervisor would linger after dinner to watch it with them.

And the highlight of the evening was the new staff, Valerie. She was a hot looking 24-year-old who was distracting a lot of the men in the house, including JJ. She thought JJ's eyes were "gorgeous" and ruffled his hair every time she walked by him. She winked at him and occasionally flirted with him. He knew it was for his satisfaction, not because she had any interest in him, but he was ok with that. Supervisor had pulled her into the office one day because she thought Valerie "might be behaving in a way that caused the wrong kind of attention on the part of our male individuals". He suspected Maria had brought this to Supervisor's attention.

For a brief moment, JJ was glad Maria was not there that evening, for the same reason he had not wanted his mother to volunteer to chaperone middle school dances, then immediately felt guilty for the thought. But Valerie was wearing these killer jeans that were slit in various places, some of them very interesting places. And a blouse that had a big neckline that dipped low over one shoulder. He did not take his eyes off her when she was in his line of sight. He knew it was only a matter of time before Supervisor came out and gave her a sweater, and after a talk in the office tonight the blessed pants would never be seen again at work.

Dinner was running late, so Joe announced he was going to take a break before dinner started. He was on a new diet so he wouldn't be joining the others for dinner anyway. JJ didn't really care, but it did mean he'd probably eat a little late, because one of the things Joe was slow at was coming back from break. No problem, he would just hang out with the staff and enjoy the glory that was Valerie.

As Joe was about to leave, he glanced at JJ and said, "Sorry J, I didn't do a very good job getting you into the chair today, did I?" Dutifully, before leaving for his break, he removed JJ's tray and turned the chair around, so he would have room to drop the back. The chair back reclined a full 180", and without too much effort staff could remove his seat belt, hook their hands under JJ's arm pits, and yank him back a few inches. The seat belt was fastened, the chair back was then raised, the tray put back on and Voila! Good as new. JJ had not realized that he had been slouching and felt the improvement, thankful that Joe had taken the time to fix him. He would enjoy his meal more if correctly positioned, and he was looking forward to this particular dinner.

Joe said, "back in 30" and walked away.

JJ gasped, 'What the hell???? Joe! No!!! Turn me around! JOE! Don't leave me like this! JOE!'

His internal voice was so shrill he couldn't believe it couldn't be heard by anyone else. 'Joe*!!!!!!!*'

He heard Joe coming back...he must have remembered...Thank God...

"Forgot my phone" Joe said to JJ without glancing up and left again.

JJ was apoplectic. He was angrier than he had been since the other night with Jason. OK, that was only a few days ago, and maybe that meant he got angry often, but still, 'What the Fuck? Who turns someone to face the wall and walks away? He knew he had probably just forgotten; he knew Joe was not mean-spirited, but Damn! The wall!?!'

As his anger seethed and he came to grips with the situation, a new level of fury erupted when he realized that he was not facing just a wall, he was facing Michael's butt! The nurse had ordered that Michael be put down prone over a foam wedge with his butt up because of a reddened area. So there Michael lay, with his butt exposed in all its glory, covered only by a single sheet! While Valerie was behind him, with her butt covered in only a flimsy web of cotton fibers when she bent over and the slits in her pants lined up just right. He was beyond furious.

When he calmed a little, he did what he always did when he felt wronged. He plotted revenge against the transgressor. Stupid Joe. Idiot Joe. Fat Joe. And to think JJ had thought he could trust him. He hoped the new diet didn't work and he continued to have to make his pathetic skinny ankles carry all that weight till he couldn't walk anymore. He hoped that Supervisor caught him coming back late from break and wrote him up. He was not any better than Jason; even if this wasn't malicious, it was neglectful. Every time he heard laughter behind him JJ became more enraged. Sure, laugh amongst yourself while I'm facing this WALL!!! And Michael's BUTT! He could hear Valerie teasing that new guy who moved in last week, he couldn't remember his name. Sure, kick me to the curb why don't you? It is bad enough Stupid Joe puts me in front of Michael's butt, but not one of you cares enough to turn me around. It would take you 30 Frigg in' seconds! You can't do that for me?

JJ could feel his pulse racing and his breathing labored. His internal rant continued for what seemed like an eternity. He remembered everything Joe had ever screwed up. The time he made hamburgers and fries and then realized there was no ketchup! Who does that? The time his car wouldn't start-and it was parked in the unloading space and for a whole day the vans had to unload in the rain because of his stupidity and his stupid rattletrap of a car. The time he wore that tee shirt that was too short, and his fat gut hung out only he didn't know it till Supervisor told him and he had to go home and change. It was amazing he was still working here.

Oh sure, most of the time he was a nice guy, and everybody liked him, and he did a good job, but still, a WALL Joe? And a Butt?

By the time Joe returned 35 minutes later, JJ was red faced and perspiring. "Sorry JJ. Didn't mean to leave you looking at a wall while I was gone." Joe turned him around and placed him at the table to eat.

As Joe turned to get his meal ready, he glanced at JJ and stopped dead. "JJ! What's wrong, Bud?" To the staff "Guys did anything happen to JJ. He looks sick!" Valerie and Julie shook their heads, and Supervisor came right over.

JJ wanted the supervisor to see how negligent Joe had been and he wanted Joe to know how much he despised him at this moment. He curled his lip as fiercely as he could. He squinted his eyes tightly and glared at Joe so Supervisor would have no question about whom to blame for this. He clenched the few muscles he still commanded in his left arm and hand and gritted his teeth. This infraction must be punished! Saying "sorry bud" wasn't going to cut it! The response he got from Supervisor and Joe was alarm. Instead of the obvious reaction that anyone could have reasonably expected, that Joe be humiliated and contrite, and Supervisor be angry and punishing, they responded with *Concern*. He didn't want concern, he wanted revenge!

"I've never seen him like this!" Supervisor said.

Joe said "He was fine when I left. Even seemed happy."

Miriam, the little old lady who lived across the hall from JJ looked up and spoke up, "He's mad."

"He's not mad." Supervisor said. "What does he have to be mad about?"

Joe worried, "I repositioned him just before I went to break. I hope I didn't pinch him when I put the tray on.

"He was looking at me like he wanted something before." Valerie offered.

Supervisor looked at her and snarled, "yeah we'll talk about that later."

JJ thought 'Damn! There goes the pants and the blouse! Won't see them again.'

Miriam said, "He's just mad."

'YES!!! I'm mad! I have every right to be mad! JJ thought. How does Miriam know that and no one else does?'

Supervisor said "Miriam stop that. JJ is ill right now and he doesn't need you saying mean things."

'I AM MAD!!!' JJ shrieked to himself.

Supervisor told Joe to put him to bed. She was going to call the nurse.

JJ screamed in his head 'NOOOOO! My pork chops!'

"And take his temperature. And check his bowel chart. Maybe he needs a laxative."

'Please! NO!' JJ began to cry with frustration.

Joe was miserable. "J, I feel so bad. I wish I knew what's hurting you, Bud. I wish I hadn't gone to dinner."

"Nothing hurts him. He's mad." Miriam said. No one ever listened to Miriam.

Back in the room Joe continued to speak to J in a kind caring tone. At first it made JJ even angrier, but then JJ began to realize he had been over- reacting just a little bit. It was really an oversight. Joe didn't mean it. And it was only a half hour. And Michael did have a sheet covering him. If he had relaxed and just waited, he'd be out there getting his dinner and glimpsing Valerie every time she crossed his path. He wouldn't be facing solitary confinement for the evening. His body unclenched as he accepted the hopelessness of the situation. Joe mistook it as relief. "There you go Bud; you look better already. Try to rest. I'll look in on you in a bit. As he left, he reached up and turned on JJ's tv. Jeopardy was on next, which relieved JJ somewhat-at least the night wouldn't be a total loss.

Supervisor came back with an Ensure pudding and a thermometer. She placed the thermometer in JJ's mouth and called out to Joe "tell the nurse it's normal." He heard Miriam say from the dining room, "Told you. He's just mad."

"Don't listen to Miriam, JJ." Supervisor said as she tucked him in after giving him pudding.

"Feel better sweetheart." She said as left, turning off his TV, "get some rest."

He closed his eyes in defeat.

CHAPTER 9

By morning he was feeling better. Although his rage had cost him a great meal, he hadn't lost everything. The menu would roll around to pork chops next month. He heard staff say that Jeopardy Champion Brendan Tyler had lived to fight another day, so tonight's episode would be equally exciting. And Valerie looked like the kind of girl who had other inappropriate clothes, so the loss of one outfit was not that big a deal. Once he calmed down, he realized it had really been his fault. His mother always said his temper would be the death of him. But the frustration he felt sometimes was so horrible he thought his head would explode.

He lay in bed, and when he heard Franklin come in, he opened his eyes as he heard, "JJ My man!"

Franklin was in a great mood, humming some new song, juggling the hygiene supplies as he prepared for morning hygiene, and checking his image out in the mirror. JJ had heard the women staff comment on Franklin's good looks, and he could see it. He used to be known to play around, but since this new girl came into his life that had all ended. Derrick complained constantly about Franklin being held captive at home.

Franklin would just laugh and say, "Maybe, but have you seen my jailor? Sweeeeet!"

JJ assumed the beach vacation had been a success, with or without the beach.

"Triple J, what's this about you not feeling well? You look fine to me! I was going to try to get you and me away from this place and go somewhere today, but they say you got to wait another day. Too damn bad!"

'Would the karma never stop?', JJ thought to himself.

Miriam who was sitting in her doorway across the hall said, "He wasn't sick he was mad." JJ shook his finger at her and said, "Now Miss Miriam you need to mind your own business." She grinned at him. She flirted shamelessly with Franklin. The little woman couldn't be more than 4' 5", and while she used a wheelchair, she could pull herself around with her feet and could stand to transfer to the bed and chairs. She and JJ had a mixed relationship. He found her very perceptive at times, but she was often up in everyone's business.

Franklin shut the door and began to get JJ ready for the day. "Got both my boys today." He said, nodding towards Wayne. "The three of us goanna' hang. Triple J, Franklin, and Bruce Wayne." That was a new nickname for Wayne, and Franklin was proud of himself.

"My man Wayne doesn't feel great lately. What's going on with you Bruce? You got me worried." Wayne didn't give any indication that he heard him, but Franklin continued anyway.

Franklin chattered on about the weekend he'd had with his lady. In the end he had to spend some time on the beach, his girl insisted on it, but they had plenty of time to surf the sheets too. Did the boys ever have lobster? It's great on the Cape, in the water in the morning, on your plate in the evening. Someday he'd take them both to Red Lobster and they could try it themselves.

Breakfast was oatmeal and fruit, with a cup of coffee to help them wake up. Not all staff thought to bring coffee, but Franklin always did, and it was always exactly like JJ liked it. Light with two sugars. He was supposed to have artificial sugar, but Franklin thought a little of the good stuff wouldn't hurt, so he always used real sugar.

After breakfast Franklin took them outside to work on the garden. Last year they had put in some vegetables and had gotten a kick out of tasting tomatoes off the vine, watching him dig potatoes, carrots, and such.

JJ had done some gardening when he was younger with his Dad. For a couple of years, they had fresh vegetables throughout the summer. He wasn't big on greens but had to admit they were pretty good fresh. Franklin raked the old plants and bagged them in a bag attached to Wayne's tray, which he put Wayne's arm on and asked him to hold. JJ could see it was tied on so it wouldn't go anywhere, but Wayne seemed to take his responsibility seriously and tried his best to hold it. It was a hot afternoon, and both he and Wayne were wearing a broad brimmed fisherman's hat and lathered up in sunscreen. JJ breathed in the earthy smell of the garden and the coconut lotion melting on his skin, and it brought back some nice memories of fishing trips and gardening and days at the lake.

Franklin prattled on about the garden, bringing some of last year's carrots that had never been harvested to show JJ and Wayne, pointing out birds who were visiting the bird feeder and naming them. JJ suspected he was making up some of the names. "Yeah, that there, is a black striped woodpecker, that's what that is." JJ was pretty sure it was a sparrow.

It didn't matter. Hanging with Franklin and Bruce Wayne. Good times!

After lunch Franklin took them to their room and put them to bed for some positioning. "To get you off your asses for a while" Franklin whispered to them and laughed at his own joke. Wayne fell asleep almost immediately, but Franklin sat next to JJ and showed him the beach pictures on his phone.

His girlfriend was pretty, and Franklin looked sharp sitting next to her with their coffee colored skin offset with the crisp white of their clothing and the tablecloth, and the pop of red that JJ assumed must be the newly deceased lobster. They looked like an advertisement for a Caribbean vacation.

JJ had been to the ocean a couple of times. He remembered it being a very emotional experience, seeing the enormity of it, the permanence of it. He had done cartwheels on the beach, swam in the surf, played frisbee with his Dad. His mom was always taking pictures. He wondered what had happened to them. He would love to have a couple to remember those days. Pictures were hard to come by since he came to live here. Privacy concerns meant it was a hassle to get permission to take pictures, there had to be consent, and with an absent father and no way to give permission himself, he was not having many selfies. It didn't matter, he had no social media to post on anyway.

The door opened and Gary the Grifter (JJ came up with that himself) came in, and Franklin immediately left. He had no use for Wayne's "loving brother".

JJ couldn't see Gary, but he heard him. No nonsense, straight to the bedside table, heard the straw being shoved in the opening.

He heard Wayne stir and heard some sucking sounds on the straw. He was not drinking fast enough-and Gary whispered,

"Come on you little bastard. Drink. I've got things to do." JJ's blood began to boil.

There was a knock on the door and Nurse Ratchet came in. JJ didn't think that was her real name but that's what Franklin called the new part time nurse. She motioned for Gary to join her in the hall, but JJ could hear everything, and he was pretty sure Wayne could too.

"We're pretty concerned about Wayne", she told him. He seems to have no stamina, by dinner he barely has the energy to eat. He's been tested for a number of things but so far we haven't gotten answers".

Gary's voice became very somber. "I am also concerned. I see him slipping a bit every week. I promised my mother I would always look after him when she couldn't any longer. Is there anything we should be doing?"

"I think we're doing all we can, but we wanted to let you know the doctor is recommending a gastro tube for feeding, just until we can diagnose the problem. He can still have real food, but we need to keep his nutrition up at the same time. The Doctor is also asking if you would mind not bringing the shake every day. Instead we could give you a supplemental shake to give him which would be more nutritious. We can't afford to waste the empty calories, and you said he seems less interested in the chocolate shakes anyway." She said all this quickly, like she thought he might object. But he was fine with the new arrangement. "Of course, I enjoy treating him, but I have to put his needs ahead of mine." He said sanctimoniously. JJ couldn't tell from her voice whether Nurse Ratchet was buying his bullshit.

"Ok then I will get some paperwork together so you can sign your approval. Thank you." She said with a bit of professional coolness.

When he came back in the room Gary took out his phone and punched a couple of numbers. "Hi, it's definitely working. He's weaker so they are putting him on a g tube. Some tube that goes into his stomach. No, it's not going to make things harder, it should make things easier. No, don't worry about that, they love me. I wouldn't be surprised if they name the place after me." He laughed to himself as he hung up, then paused for a minute as he caught JJ staring. They stared each other down for a moment, but he was the one who broke eye contact.

"You sick, little busy body" he whispered to JJ, then collected his things without so much as a glance towards Wayne. As he left, he deliberately banged into JJ's bed to startle him.

CHAPTER 10

4:15 came without the usual anticipation. JJ had convinced himself Maria would be out today so he would not be disappointed. But there she was, with a cheery greeting, but with the signs of a bruised face under her makeup and a troubled look in her eyes.

"How's my guy?" She asked, sounding exhausted. "I heard you had a rough night. You have to get along with other staff when I'm not here, Carino. You can't be upset if I'm off. Promise you'll try." She held his face in her hands. "Not that awful Jason, but Joe is very kind and he likes you very much. He felt very bad last night."

JJ just smiled and relaxed. Sweet Maria.

It was a sunny day, so Maria took JJ for a walk before dinner. The spring flowers were starting to pop up, and the trees had subtle green buds if you saw them up close. They walked by the dog who barked a hello, and Maria greeted him. The more they walked the more relaxed Maria became. She hummed a Spanish song she said her mother used to sing to her. She walked along next to J and steered the wheelchair with one hand when they are on level ground.

As they rounded the third corner of the block, a blue car came around the corner, a Civic, JJ thought. It passed them, then slammed on the brakes. The driver threw it in reverse and the car screeched backwards. JJ caught a glimpse of the driver- a thirty something guy who looked like he wanted to hit something.

"Maria, I just want to talk to you." The man, who JJ presumed was Brad, said in a syrupy voice. He left the car and strode toward them. JJ felt very intimated.

Maria shook with fear, "I'm at work Brad. Not now. I'll call you later." And she quickened her pace.

"That's what you said the other night. And did you?" Brad's tone was menacing, and his stride was steady as he approached.

"I hate when you do this to me Maria. Then you wonder why I lose my temper." His stride was faster now, and he was almost on them.

Maria gasped "Oh God Help Me!" She leaned on the wheelchair and they raced the last couple hundred feet to the house. A grey-haired man in front of them, the next-door neighbor JJ believed, looked up from his mailbox, and yelled "You! Leave them alone or I'll call the police!" Maria ran past him and JJ heard the neighbor step behind them, blocking Brad. JJ worried that the old man would be hurt, but after hearing some hurled insults the door slammed again and the car sped off. Maria yelled a thank you to the man as they made it to the house.

Inside the house Maria collapsed in a chair and sobbed. Julia shouted "Mona!" And supervisor came running. Between sobs Maria told her what had happened. Mona bolted the front door and called the police, asking them to patrol the area, then put an arm around Maria and guided her to the office.

Julia took JJ under her wing and got him dinner, but he didn't have much of an appetite. Never had he felt the terror he had today. His stomach clenched and his heart pounded.

The evening was somber. There was a movie, though JJ couldn't tell you which one. Maria came out of the office after a while and tried to put on a brave face but would soon become tearful and excuse herself again. Supervisor asked if she wanted to go home, but she begged not to. All doors were locked, and staff were told if Maria's boyfriend Brad were to be spotted the police were to be called immediately.

At bedtime as Maria got JJ ready for bed, she tried to lighten the mood. "JJ you need a haircut! Franklin will take you. Do you remember when Mona took you? You ended up looking like an Army recruit! You need a cool haircut. What do they call the one that swoops to the side? That would be nice," and she brushed his hair to one side with her fingers. But her eyes were dark pools of sorrow.

Around 10 o'clock, long after Maria had kissed his forehead good night, JJ lay staring at the ceiling. He heard the door open and saw Maria's face above him, still sad, but also concerned.

"JJ, can't sleep? She patted his hand and fluffed his pillow. "I feel I owe you an explanation. I'm sorry that happened to you today. I never want to bring my problems to work. You have your own problems; you don't need mine too. But I want you to know it will not happen again. That man is Brad, my boyfriend, or my ex-boyfriend. He has been hurting me, and last week he hit me harder than he ever has, and I left, and he is very angry about it. Tomorrow I will go to court and get a restraining order, so he won't bother me anymore. I don't want you to worry because it won't happen again. Julie is taking me home with her, and her husband is picking us up. Her husband is a cop, JJ, and he is as big as a refrigerator! Brad would not mess with him!" she smiled. "I am so lucky to have you all in my life. We are one big family, JJ, and we will take care of each other. And I promise I will not let anything like that happen to you again.

CHAPTER 11

The next morning dawned with a charcoal sky and JJ knew he was stuck inside. Franklin was his staff today, which was good because sometimes he was most creative on days like this. They could end up on an outing or watching a bootleg video or making a volcano with vinegar and baking soda (though Supervisor had told him if he ever made a mess like that again she would give him kitchen duty for a month.)

At 8:00, Supervisor came in. She said Franklin was giving meds, so she was going to help JJ get up and ready for breakfast. That was odd- Franklin gave meds a few times a week and he never needed help taking care of his people. She got JJ ready for his day and brought him to the table in the dining room and he could feel a bit of tension. There was no chatter between staff. Staff spoke to their people in soft tentative voices, choosing their words carefully. As JJ was pushed up to the table, it all started to make sense. Across from him was a woman in a beige suit, with a name tag on her lapel and a clipboard in her hand, with a blank look on her face. An auditor. They were being audited. JJ's lip curled up in a smile. These were usually amusing days.

Franklin came to JJ with the medication cart. He usually just brought the cup of pills to the table. He looked at the orders, looked at the labels, looked at the orders again, counted the pills in the cup; just like they do when new staff were learning to do meds. He was following protocol. Since he rarely followed protocol, he was very awkward about it.

He was supposed to check the order against the prescription against the bottle: a triple check. Maybe to make up for not having done it since the last audit, he repeated the sequence a dozen times to be sure. He then very formally said "Mr. Johnson, I have your meds for you." JJ wished he was able to turn his head- he would have looked behind himself to see who Franklin was talking to: *Mr. Johnson?*

JJ had a medication goal to take his medications with water instead of applesauce. He was perfectly capable of taking his pills with water, but why, when he could get a cup of applesauce added to his meal? The Dietician was stingy with food. Take extra when you can get it! But today Franklin would be giving him water.

"Mr. Johnson, here is your Omeprazole and Vitamin D", He said to JJ, with formality that made Supervisor, who was behind the auditor, cover her mouth to suppress a laugh. JJ took the pills from the cup and started to push them out with his tongue, just to mess with Franklin, but he was so nervous JJ took pity on him and swallowed them. Franklin was going to have a long shift.

Before long, breakfast was over and the voice was droning on again, "The Robin, sometimes called Robin Red Breast, is one of the first birds to arrive in the spring...." As usual his peers were settling in for a nap. This was not a popular activity. They used to have a whole set of nature DVD's, but someone had put the case of them on top of the bookshelf. The shelf was bumped, and the case fell behind the bookcase. The only one who knew this was JJ, who had seen it happen, but he had no way to tell anyone. So, when the schedule said Nature Videos, they were left with the one left in the machine.

JJ wondered why they had never got to watch the Discovery Channel. He used to love it as a kid. Then one day a staff asked Mona if they could watch Discovery instead, and she was told that watching Discovery would count as television. The agency had a policy that limited them to two hours of television a day. The DVD's were a different category of activity-educational, and so they could spend the useless hour in front of the television without violating the policy. The house was doomed to watch robins until they did the next deep clean when staff moved the bookcase.

Mona whispered something to poor Gina, the shy night shift staff who got stuck doing overtime. Gina was not too familiar with typical day time routine, much less audit routine. She was a trooper and got up, took her charges to the kitchen and before long they were making cookies for tonight's dessert. JJ was a little sullen because he loved working in the kitchen.

JJ decided he wouldn't play the game and shut his eyes tight and ignored the movie. Franklin came to sit next to him and nervously tried to engage JJ in the video.

"See that J? Remember when we worked in the garden? We saw a robin, didn't we J?

JJ kept his eyes closed, but his lip curled up slightly and Franklin saw it.

"Look J look! The mom is feeding the baby a worm. We saw worms in the garden yesterday, didn't we? We sure did!" He was tapping JJ's arm and lifting his chin towards the screen. JJ knew the auditor was still there because of Franklin's frantic attempts. But he kept his eyes shut and let Franklin hang out there a little longer. He heard a chair scrape and opened his eyes to see the auditor head to the kitchen to look into the cooking class. Franklin leaned close to JJ and whispered,

"Don't do this to me J. If you keep messing with me, I swear to God I'll never show you another bootleg movie again. No siree. Never!"

JJ's lip curled up even further and he shut his eyes. An empty threat- Franklin liked seeing them as much as he did. Franklin's foot was nervously tapping. "J, I been good to you. Don't do this to me man."

He heard the woman's voice commenting on the cooking group, then footsteps getting closer....

Again, Franklin leaned in, "Okay, okay, if you pretend to watch the movie, I'll bring you a milkshake from McDonald's tomorrow." JJ's eyes popped open. Franklin looked so relieved. "See J, that's how they make their nests," he said, pointing to the video. JJ's gaze followed with rapt attention. A shake, eh? It had been a while.

The morning went well after that. Franklin couldn't wait to get JJ into bed for his scheduled positioning. While Franklin used the lift, the auditor went through JJ's dresser and Wayne's and looked at labels and counted shorts and shirts and socks. She found a pair of JJ's socks in Wayne's dresser and wrote something down on paper.

"Don't worry, it's just a pair of socks, Franklin whispered to JJ. "They won't make a big deal out of a pair of socks."

At lunchtime, Franklin gave JJ his drink in the blue cut out cup he always used. A cut-out cup is a cup that has a section cut out for a person's nose, so that when the cup is tipped the staff can see the liquid and avoid making the individual extend his or her neck backwards to get the liquid. It's a piece of adaptive equipment that an occupational therapist chooses. JJ didn't feel he needed it, but his therapist did, so there you are. The auditor asked why it had Wayne's name on it.

"Oh, goodness, did I grab the wrong cup? Let me see where JJ's cup is. It's the same color. My mistake."

Franklin hurried off to the kitchen, to look for a cup that both he and JJ knew had melted in the dishwasher months ago. He came back and earnestly said "....so, I believe this is JJ's cup. The OT is always giving the guys nicknames, and I believed she nick-named JJ Wayne, and I think that is why his cup says Wayne. I'm pretty sure that's why. I will ask her when I see her, but I think I've heard her call JJ Wayne, like in John Wayne..."

JJ thought Franklin looked like he might be sick.

At this point Supervisor came over with a black permanent marker. She crossed out Wayne and wrote JJ on the cup. "JJ's cup melted in the dishwasher. Wayne was put on a straw by the Occupational Therapist, so he no longer uses this cup, JJ does." She said matter of factly.

The auditor just said thank you and that was that.

After lunch JJ went into repositioning with Wayne, the auditor went to the office to look at files, and Franklin took a much-needed break.

JJ's eyes closed for a little while, but he woke when the door was opened, and Gary came in.

JJ listened carefully and fixed his eyes to the left as far as he could. He could see just a bit of Gary's shoulder and head. He had the Ensure given to him by staff and JJ heard the pop of the tab, but he did not give any to Wayne. JJ heard him pour the contents down the sink. He mumbled "You don't need that. You get that tube tomorrow and after that things should move quickly."

He left after a few minutes. In the hall, JJ heard the auditor speak to him, probably to find out what he thought of the place. He uttered a couple of superlatives and was gone.

After positioning Supervisor sent Franklin and JJ for a long walk in a last-ditch effort to avoid Franklin having a complete melt-down. The other staff were much calmer than he was. On the walk Franklin vented to JJ.

"I don't know why they make me so nervous. I do a good job. I think we have a good house and Mona is a good supervisor. I just don't want to be the one to mess up and cause a problem. You know what I mean J? I'd feel like I let everybody down. And, you know, I might want to move up someday."

In the end the house did fine, they received only accolades for how well staff interacted with the residents, and a warning that there were a couple of cereal boxes beyond the expiration date in the cupboard.

Franklin left saying he was going to stop on the way home to get a six pack.

CHAPTER 12

The surgery to place Wayne's gastro tube was the next day, and while one might think a concerned brother would want to check on him, Gary did not reappear for two days.

When he did, JJ was once again positioned on his side. Gary must have decided JJ posed no threat because his wariness around him was gone. He came in, popped the top of the Ensure, poured a little down the drain of the sink. He picked up the tube and examined it. Wayne was given "bolus feedings", which basically means the cap is popped up, and nutritional liquid is poured into the tube directly into the stomach, which both spared the fatigue that came with eating and ensured it was not lost through spills. Wayne could eat what he wanted to by mouth to supplement it. If Wayne improved the tube could be removed. JJ didn't think Gary planned on him improving.

Gary looked it over, then popped the cap of the tube, glanced at the door to make sure he was alone, removed a syringe from his pocket, and plunged it into the tube. He then recapped the tube and left without a glance at Wayne or JJ.

CHAPTER 13

Maria was in the next day at 7:00. JJ was confused when he saw her, he expected Franklin. She laughed, "Did I surprise you? Well, let me tell you what is happening" she began to do JJ's morning routine as she chattered. "I am switching shifts for a little while with Franklin. He will work evenings for me, and I will work mornings for him. That way I can come to work with Julie since she and her husband are letting me live with them for a while. I am so grateful that all of them are helping me. And I still get to spend time with you!"

For an instant he was taken aback by the thought that she would ever *not* be able to spend time with him. It hadn't occurred to him. She seemed very relieved, and JJ was happy that Maria was happy.

The day was fun. They started off in the kitchen, making cookies for the neighbor who had been such a hero the other night. After lunch, they took a walk and stopped at his house, this time with a few others along for safety. Then back to the room for repositioning. Gary was at Wayne's bed when they got there, and he was startled when Maria pushed the door open. He stuffed something back in his pocket and dropped the gastro tube. For an awkward moment no one spoke, then Maria asked stiffly "Can I help with something? Is there a problem with his tube?".

Gary glared and said, "No, if I need information about his tube, I'll ask the nurse, thank you". He stiffly left the room without eye contact with anyone. The room had a medicine smell, but JJ doubted Maria would notice. Maria left JJ next to his bed and walked over to Wayne's bed. She stroked his head and felt his forehead. "You alright Wayne? Why are you feeling so sick lately?" She looked down at the gastro tube. "Oh dear! Mona!"

Supervisor came running and looked at the gastro tube which was uncapped and leaking. The nurse was called, and Maria explained what she'd seen. They discussed it and decided Gary was just being curious and was too embarrassed to admit it. He probably meant no harm. JJ knew better but couldn't say. As they cleaned up the mess, Maria said to Supervisor, "What food is he getting? It doesn't smell like the formula that's used for Michael."

"Don't ask me, I can't smell a thing." Supervisor waved away the question.

Maria was not convinced of Gary's innocence, JJ could tell. With a thoughtful look Maria helped JJ into bed. "Something is going on, JJ." She said, not expecting a response.

After lunch, some people went on walks, some went to the back yard, and some went to their rooms. JJ went out to the back yard with Maria and spent his 30-minutes upright enjoying the sunshine. Maria was not diligent with the 30-minute rule and lingered a little longer, seeing how much JJ was enjoying being outside.

"Ok, J, I've delayed long enough. You have to get into bed for a little while before your skin gets red."

She stood up and began to unlatch his brakes, when JJ's heart quickened at the sight of Brad standing behind her.

"I didn't get that phone call last night Maria. Playing me for a fool?" He growled and grabbed her arm. She gasped and struggled against his grip.

"Brad you have to go! You'll get me fired!" Maria whimpered.

"That's supposed to bother me? You little whore. All the time I spent on you and you treat me like this. Then you want everyone to feel bad for you!" His hand on her arm tightened and JJ could see the pain in her face. JJ's face went red with rage, and Brad noticed and laughed at him.

"This your new boyfriend? Pathetic." He sneered, enjoying her pain.

At that point the voices of the walkers were heard coming up the side of the house, and Maria pulled away as Brad took a step backwards. Maria took JJ's chair and quickly went to the back door, fumbling with the key as her hands trembled uncontrollably.

"Call me." Brad called out to her in a mocking tone.

Maria's voice trembled when they got inside.

"Don't worry JJ, don't worry. I'll call my lawyer and try to get my court hearing pushed up. Don't worry. He is just trying to intimidate me. It will be fine." She stammered, but the one thing JJ was sure it would not be, was fine.

CHAPTER 14

The next morning Maria seemed better. She was relaxed, laughing, singing. The lawyer had communicated his intent to have Brad arrested for harassment if he didn't leave her alone, and she had her court date pushed up to the next day. She told Julie she felt almost free.

When Maria was happy, she brought the best out in everyone in the house. She made home-made biscuits for breakfast, fresh strawberries for lunch. They went outside and filled the bird feeders, then sat in the yard and watched the birds eat. She taught Miriam, who was able to use her hands, to take a picture with her cell phone. They listened to Latin music after lunch while clean-up was done, then she took JJ back to his room. Wayne was gone to a medical appt, so there would be no visitor today.

After putting JJ in the bed, she began to empty his urine bag, detaching the catheter and leaning the bag against his leg. She capped the catheter but before she could finish, a loud banging on the side door interrupted her. She said excuse me to JJ and went to answer it. Staff who worked in the back yard sometimes used this entrance because it was closer. JJ assumed someone had forgotten their key.

A second later Maria returned, propelled by Brad, who was holding a knife to her throat. Her eyes were wild with terror; her mouth was covered by Brad's hand, and the look on his face was murderous. JJ's heart pounded and he tried to think where others would be. Valerie was in the kitchen when they left the dining room, with the dishwasher going and the Latin music playing she wouldn't have heard anything. His peers were either in the dining room or in their rooms, and the only one who could call out would be Miriam, but she was probably sound asleep. Supervisor was on break, in her office with the door closed. The other two staff were with Wayne and the new guy at the doctors. No help would be coming.

Brad was growling horrible threats in Maria's ear, the knife centimeters from her jugular, but then they passed out of view. JJ heard Maria struggling but couldn't see. He willed his left arm to move. Adrenalin fueled his efforts and his hand touched the rail. He hooked his fingers around the rail and pulled with all his might. His body lifted slightly, and he saw Brad leaning over Maria who he had seated on Wayne's bed, trying to push her back. She struggled with him and the knife had already nicked her neck, causing a trickle of blood to run down to her neckline. Her terrified eyes screamed for help as Brad suffocated her and held the knife to her throat, almost as if deciding which death would give him more pleasure. JJ pulled on the rail and his body lifted farther than it ever had, trying to do something, though he had no idea what. As his body moved upward, and to the left, his leg rotated as well, and the urine bag which was leaning against his leg tipped off the bed, splattering urine on Brad's legs and feet. He was startled and yelled "Fuck!" and in that instant Maria rolled out of his grasp, screamed as loud as she could and ran to the door. JJ's strength was exhausted, and he fell back onto the bed. Brad grabbed her by the hair and dragged her back to the bed, but he was disgusted by the urine splashing on his shoes and heard someone call out "everything ok?" In fury, he shoved Maria down in the puddle and ran out the back just before Mona got to the door. Maria sat in a trembling heap of misery, sobbing.

CHAPTER 15

The rest of the evening was surreal. The police came. They took Maria to the station. Staff talked in the hall about the incident, nervously wondering if Brad had been arrested yet. At one point he heard Jason venture a weak defense of Brad, saying she must have done something to really piss him off, and from their voices JJ thought Jason might need protection from Julie and Valerie. JJ prayed with all his might that Maria was alright. Staff kept coming in to check on him and asking how he was doing, but JJ thought even if he had his voice, he would be at a loss to even try to communicate what he was feeling.

JJ had seen such scenes in tv shows and movies when he lived at home, but he never would have believed someone could be capable of inflicting such harm on another, certainly not someone who was once a lover. JJ's heart broke to think of the pain Maria must be in, to have so much hatred and anger directed at her.

There was no pleasure in the house that evening. The joy that he had felt all morning was replaced with a somber tension that continued till bedtime, which, that night, couldn't come fast enough.

CHAPTER 16

Not surprisingly Maria was not in the next day. Franklin came in for her shift, and while he tried to keep things light, he was preoccupied, just like Supervisor and the other staff. They had breakfast and since it was raining, they all watched, or slept through the nature video. Franklin sat next to JJ and let him close his eyes and nap for a while, but Franklin was nervous, sitting on the edge of his seat and fidgeting. Finally, he said,

"Hey, Triple J, you awake man? I want to talk to you for a minute if that's ok. Is that ok? I just want to say, what happened yesterday, that's just sick man, and I'm sorry you had to see that, but I hear you basically saved Maria's life, which is amazing man. You're a hero JJ. But I know that must have been freaky to see that, and I know you can't talk about it, but I want you to know I'm here for you man." JJ opened his eyes, and tried to curl his lip in acknowledgement, and though he tried to stop it, a tear squeezed out and trickled down his cheek. Franklin stood up and wrapped his arms around him and hugged him. For once, Franklin was lost for words.

CHAPTER 17

Th+at afternoon Gary came and strode into the room like he owned it.

He was talking on the phone when he came in, and lowered his voice, checking the bathroom to be sure no one was listening. JJ believed it was the same person he overheard Gary speak to the first time.

"What did the doctor say? Yeah, six months is what he said six months ago. Was he surprised her sugars were high? That's what I figured; they will assume it's the cancer...No, there isn't a lot of pain for her or him. I'm not a monster. But listen, now that he's got a tube, I think I'm going to stay with Tetra hydroxide, but hold on to that insulin just in case. It's quick, and since he's been failing. I don't think a sudden death will be surprising. If they ask for an autopsy, we say no. We need to set a date for him, and then when we're sure we're in the clear, set a date for Mother. And then life will return to normal.... Don't get all moral on me little brother. She has no quality of life anymore, and Wayne has no life to speak of anyway. You and I are not taking anything of value from either of them. And if a third of her estate goes to him the State will just take it. Damned if I let that happen."

Off the phone, JJ couldn't see what Gary was doing but he knew, nonetheless. Now that he didn't need the ruse of the chocolate shake, he would just inject into the tube and be gone, without a hello or goodbye for Wayne.

JJ was stunned. He had suspected that Gary was harming Wayne, but now it was confirmed, and he felt the weight of this knowledge on his chest. What could he do? What kind of date did they have in mind? Was it imminent? He shuddered to think he could be forced to watch Wayne be killed right in front of him and not be able to help him. He would not be sleeping easily tonight.

CHAPTER 18

Franklin was in for Maria the next day also but was much more his usual self. He told JJ that Maria had called and said that Brad had been arrested, and she wanted JJ to know that he was safe and so was she. She was not hurt but was taking a few days to rest. It was a hot day for April 28th, and Franklin said "Let's get you in some shorts. It's 79 degrees out there, J!"

He fumbled in the closet, muttering.

"I thought you got some new clothes, J? We got to do your laundry- or you're going to be having breakfast in your birthday suit!"

Finally, Franklin held up the denim shorts. "I hate to do this to you J, but this is all you got. Are these really a thing? I haven't seen jean shorts outside of 70s or 80s movies. Things have been so crazy lately we're way behind on everything. We'll get it caught up today. Then we can mess around tomorrow, ok Triple J?"

At breakfast Supervisor was very pleased to see JJ wearing his new shorts. She asked Franklin how they fit, and he hedged "They're ok, they fit ok. This is all he had in his closet. I have to catch up his laundry." Derrick smirked and then mouthed "sorry JJ" when he saw him. The shorts were not even the "right" shade of denim and fell to the bottom of his knee cap. JJ was mortified.

Supervisor said "Well he has the shorts and shirts I bought him. He hasn't worn them yet." Franklin shook his head "I haven't seen them."

Supervisor looked at him with surprise. When she finished breakfast with Miriam, she went back to the room to look, and did not return for a long time.

When she did return, she looked cross.

"Okay, does anyone have any ideas? They are not in any closet, dresser, hamper or laundry room. Three shirts and three shorts."

She was upset. Julie and Derrick just looked at each other, and Franklin shook his head, glancing at the two of them and then speaking for all he said,

"We don't have a clue."

Supervisor went to the office. No one said anything at first, then Julie asked meekly,

"She doesn't think we took them, does she?"

Derrick snorted, "I saw those shorts. I wouldn't wear them to wash my car." Then, to JJ, "No offense JJ."

Franklin shrugged it off, "I don't think she suspects any of us, but she has to put in a report, because they didn't just disappear. We never had theft here like some of the houses. Mona runs a tight ship. That's why I like working here. Don't worry about it, maybe they'll turn up."

Franklin surprised JJ with that statement since from JJ's perspective Franklin did the best, he could to poke holes in Mona's "tight ship".

At lunch Franklin spilled JJ's drink on his wheelchair tray, and some of the liquid ended up in JJ's lap.

"Sorry J. Good thing I got your laundry caught up this morning, eh?"

He took JJ back to his room and put him into bed. He removed the shorts and turned to put some fresh athletic pants on when he froze. He looked at JJ's legs, which of course JJ couldn't see, then looked at his face. "You ok J? Nothing hurts, right?" JJ just looked at him, confused. "I'll be right back." He covered JJ with a sheet and went to get Supervisor.

Supervisor came back looking harried. She flipped back the sheet and gasped. "Oh my God. JJ, what happened to you?" She helped Franklin turn JJ to his side and said "they're all over. Like he fell out of bed and rolled or something."

Supervisor looked at Franklin, "But he was with you!"

Franklin looked defensive "I know! Nothing happened! Maybe they were there this morning and got darker! I don't think I put the light on, maybe that's why I didn't see them. Nothing happened!"

She looked totally overwhelmed. "I haven't even finished the incident report for the stolen clothes and now this. What is going on?" She left and Franklin stood looking helpless. After a while he said to JJ, "I guess I should tell you what we're looking at JJ. You got bruises all over your thighs. They look bad, not little ones like if you bumped your leg on the chair or nothing, big ones, everywhere. I don't know why I didn't see them this morning. Maybe because I didn't turn the light on? I wish you could tell us what happened. Well get some rest. I'll talk to you in a little while."

Not twenty minutes later Nurse Ratchet (her real name was Molly) came and kept a neutral face while examining the bruises. Supervisor came with her and took some pictures with a digital camera, then hurried off to send them to the investigators. Molly told Franklin to get JJ ready to go to the ER.

"JJ, I don't know if you remember me. I'm Molly, the nurse. We need to have you go to the ER and find out where all these bruises came from and whether you're hurt anywhere."

She didn't wait for a response.

Ok, well JJ was totally mystified but what the hell? Another trip to the ER with Franklin. Sweet! He hoped that cute little nurse was there today. Kamisha, he thought her name was."

At the hospital he was undressed and put in an open back gown. A young resident came in and looked and poked and prodded, watching JJ's face for signs of pain. Kamisha was, in fact, there, and continued to flirt with JJ. Franklin teased her back.

The resident ordered x-rays to ensure there were no fractures and left while they were done. After a long period of time, what seemed like a very unnecessary wait, she came back to say the x-rays match his previous x-rays (JJ noted she didn't say normal). She asked again how the injury was believed to have happened and looked stone-faced while Franklin insisted no one knew. Her blank affect made him uncomfortable, and he felt pressured to add "He didn't fall, he wasn't in an altercation (JJ almost laughed at the thought of himself in an altercation), and nothing fell on him. We really don't know."

When she left, Franklin called Supervisor, "They're acting like we did something to him. This is crazy. Do you know anything yet?" He asked.

They had checked the bed rails, interviewed Joe who had worked with him the night before, interviewed Gina who had been there on the shift, even Miriam was questioned. No one had a clue.

Finally, an hour and a half later the Supervising Physician came in. He pulled back the sheet, looked at JJ, looked suspiciously at Franklin, then stood back and thought. Suddenly he took a washcloth and got it wet with hot water and soap, and scrubbed JJ's leg. Everyone gasped and looked away as the bruise disappeared in front of their eyes. The physician looked up and said, "new jeans?" Franklin looked sheepish and nodded yes.

The Doctor smirked and left. The Resident looked annoyed and walked out. Kamisha and Franklin looked at each other for a full minute, then broke down and laughed deep belly laughs. JJ smirked. It felt good to hear laughter.

CHAPTER 19

The evening was quiet and uneventful. The Jeopardy champion was back and was victorious once again. Valerie had made what turned out to be a pretty decent Lasagna (who knew she had domestic skills?), and Joe, who had relieved Franklin from doing another double shift, was good company. A welcome, peaceful, quiet evening after recent events.

Around midnight JJ woke to hear his door open and close, and his wardrobe closet door open. He couldn't see who it was because his wardrobe closet was to his right. out of his line of sight. JJ immediately tensed-after learning of Gary's plans for Wayne, JJ was on edge every time someone walked in.

A minute later the door opened again, and Joe appeared in the wedge of light from the hallway. He glanced at Wayne and at JJ, doing his regular 30-minute visual checks. He saw that JJ was awake and whispered, "hey bud" and was about to close the door when he stopped and said "oh, Gina, I didn't know you were in here. What are you doing?"

"Putting some clothes away." Gina responded.

Joe was silent for a moment, then said "oh, I thought I had gotten them all." JJ thought so too.

CHAPTER 20

The next morning, April 30th, Franklin burst into the room as usual. "Triple J! It's the end of the month and we got to do your outing today! Your lucky day! You and I are going to get out of this place. You need a haircut, gotta get us some lunch, and then we'll see what kind of time we have. Let's see what you got to wear."

JJ heard him yank the dresser drawers and a shirt landed on the bed.

Another drawer pulled open and then quiet. Then the wardrobe door opened. Again quiet. Franklin patted his ankles as he went to the door and said, "Hang tight J. Got to go find Mona."

He returned with Mona and she and he looked into the drawers and the wardrobe, and in muffled voices discussed what they found. JJ gathered that the clothes that were missing were returned. The shirts were the ones Mona had bought, but two of the shorts, while the same style, she thought might be different colors. She couldn't remember for sure.

"How very odd", Mona said. Franklin agreed. JJ was confused.

Breakfast was pancakes and sausage. It was a good thing that JJ wasn't that fond of either, because the second he hesitated on a forkful, Franklin interpreted that as satiation and packed up the meal. Franklin viewed every chance to do an outing as the ultimate road trip and couldn't wait to get started.

Mona had suggested he wear his new clothes, but Franklin said he tried one pair of the shorts on and they were a bit constricted around the waist. Maybe he should take them back and get something with an elastic waist? Supervisor seemed a bit disappointed and insulted, but she said if that's what he thought, ok, but not until the investigative team had seen them so they could wrap up the investigation. JJ smirked-he knew Franklin would have his back.

Back in the room Franklin fussed over him, putting some cologne on and gelling his hair. He had put on a T-shirt with some movie reference that Franklin had assured him was very cool, and a pair of athletic pants. He felt kind of cool. Kickin' it with Franklin, he thought as they headed out.

Franklin always took JJ to his own barber. The barber's name was Devin, and he had a little place in what Franklin said was the neighborhood he grew up in. JJ was a bit of a celebrity there. Devin made his regular customers wait when JJ arrived, but they didn't seem to mind. They were older guys, and it never looked like they were in a hurry. Franklin knew everyone, and the conversation was always lively, sometimes colorful, and while JJ didn't have a clue most of the time what they were talking about, he loved it. Devin always said, "so Triple J, what do you want me to do today?" Franklin would point out some pictures, or sometimes to the heads of those in the waiting room and ask JJ what style he wanted. JJ would draw up his lip if he saw something he liked, though a lot of the time he really didn't care and would have been happy to have Franklin pick. He generally didn't see that it made that much difference. Every now and then Franklin would suggest something that JJ wouldn't have thought of, like the time he had JJ shaved into his head. Today there was a brief discussion about dyeing it blue, but Franklin chickened out, saying he really needed to get permission to do that. JJ was a bit disappointed.

After his hair was styled, and a spirited discussion about some new boxing up and comer who either was or was not the next Holyfield, a bit of a debate over current affairs, and a bit of local gossip, Franklin ushered JJ out to the van for the second phase of his outing.

They had settled on lunch at a hamburger place that JJ had eaten at before.

They had every topping imaginable, and Franklin always read each one and waited for JJ's reaction before ordering. Franklin found it hard to interpret JJ's expression after a while, because as he tired the movement was less distinct.

"Let's try you blink once for yes, and twice for no J."

For Franklin, JJ tried, but blinking was involuntary, and while JJ could willfully blink, his response time was slow, so he was often misinterpreted.

"Ok that's not working. Have we ever tried this J? Look over here to the right for "yes". We won't worry about "no". Ok? Let's try. Grilled onions."

JJ hated onions so he stared straight ahead. "Ketchup." JJ rolled his eyes to the right as quickly as he could. Franklin said "Yeah, I got you. Ketchup it is." And continued down the list. At the end JJ had his perfect burger, Franklin ordered for himself, and they ate, Franklin taking turns putting cut up burger into JJ's mouth (minus the regulatory gloves) and taking turns eating his own sandwich, interspersing it with some of the best fries JJ ever had, with a chocolate shake to wash it down. This was way more, and way richer, food than JJ ate at a meal, and while he loved it, he was full before it was half gone.

"No problem, J, we'll take this home with us. Just give me a sec to finish eating."

JJ looked over the restaurant while Franklin finished his meal. It reminded him of Harvey's Burger Place, a place he and his friends would go to once a week back at home. His best friend back then was Jack Torrent, a kid who had been his confidant since second grade. He was the first person who JJ shared his suspicion that Santa wasn't real, he sat with him while Jack cried over a crush during fifth grade, and Jack returned the favor the day JJ learned of his mother's passing while watching Phineas and Ferb at Jack's house. Jack had come to the hospital every couple of days in the beginning, but like everyone else, the frequency just dwindled as they realized JJ would not be getting better and didn't seem to care whether they came or not. He wondered if Jack was married yet, whether he'd gone to school or just got a job, whether he had kids, did he ever remember their friendship like JJ did?

As Franklin was packing up the trash his phone rang. He answered it as he stood to get JJ ready to leave. His voice immediately became tense.

"Why does it have to be today? I told you I'm working till 11. Why are you scared? What'd he do to you? What do you mean he raised his fist? Did he ever hit you before? Why was he mad? Jesus, Krystal! I told you he was no good. Where is he? Where are you? When is he coming back? I'll give you money for a cab... How much stuff? A bed???? Leave the bed! Stop crying and listen to me! Ok, OK, I'll be there in a minute."

Off the phone, Franklin was quiet for a minute, assisting JJ out of the restaurant in silence. As the van lift lowered, he said to JJ, "Listen, bro, I'm really sorry, I have to go get my sister. She's got herself involved with this bastard, excuse my French, and I'm afraid if I don't go, he could end up hurting her. You understand J? I know you wanted to go to the movies, but I swear I'll make it up to you. I need to bring the van because she has a bed she needs to take. I can't believe she got herself in this mess. You ok with this Triple J? I really am sorry." He didn't expect an answer but was surprised when JJ looked deliberately to the right. This made Franklin stop-he wasn't used to two-way conversations. He smiled for a moment, "You know JJ, you are one of my favorite people. If I didn't work with you, I would still want to hang. You're a cool guy."

JJ thought his heart would burst.

CHAPTER 21

Franklin made a quick call to the house to tell them they would be back a little later. He was nervous. He would be fired if they ever caught him doing this. He was both angry with, and scared for, his sister

JJ had met her once when she came to the house to borrow money from Franklin. She was cute, about 21 JJ guessed, but a bit of a free spirit. She was in college for Art and was a talented painter. Franklin had shared some pictures of her work with JJ. Franklin was a very protective big brother and had been very upset when she moved in with the guy she was now leaving.

They got to the house, a small shabby place outside of town, and Krystal was waiting for them. She motioned for Franklin to follow her and he told JJ "be right back." JJ heard Franklin ask Krystal how much stuff she had to take.

"Just the bed" she said.

"Where is everything else?" Franklin stopped in his tracks.

"Mike took everything else over for me this afternoon." Krystal seemed nervous too.

"Why wouldn't he take the bed if he was willing to take everything else?" Franklin sounded confused.

"Franklin let's go before he gets home. It's just the mattress. I'll have to get a frame later."

Five minutes later Franklin appeared, struggling with the thick mattress. Krystal was behind, gingerly holding on but clearly not carrying anything. Franklin walked next to the van and JJ heard the steady stream of expletives as he labored under the heavy mattress. "Open the door!" He growled at Krystal, and she ran in front of him and threw open the back doors of the van. Franklin shoved the mattress into the van next to JJ.

The mattress almost immediately curled over and rested on JJ's head. Franklin climbed in, still sputtering his dissatisfaction with his sister's life decisions, and looked in the rearview mirror. "JJ! Are you ok? Get that mattress off him!", Franklin barked at Krystal. She wriggled around the shift and pulled the mattress up, but before she could get back into her seat, it fell back down. "You need to keep it off him! Franklin snarled at her. "I'm so sorry about all of this JJ." Krystal smiled an apology too and struggled with it for a minute before finally deciding to just hold it up herself.

"Please, Franklin, go!" she said.

She braced herself against Franklin's seat while letting the weight of the mattress rest on her back, and JJ thought it was probably the most ridiculous thing he'd ever seen. Still, she wasn't bad to look at, and truthfully this was the most fun he'd had in a long time.

Franklin got to the end of the driveway and asked, "which way?"

Krystal pointed to the left and he turned, the mattress squishing Krystal as the van rounded the turn.

After a few minutes on the road Franklin asked again, "Which way? Where are we going?"

Krystal, in a little girl's voice, said "your house".

Krystal almost fell into JJ's lap as the van screeched to a halt on the side of the road.

"Franklin, it's only for a few days till I figure something out. I promise. "I'll be out of your hair by the weekend. I swear. You won't even know I'm there!"

"No! NO! You said you were staying with a friend! No! Franklin was spitting he was so mad.

"Well you are a friend and my big brother!" Krystal tried again with her little girl's voice.

"I have a one-bedroom apartment! I share it with my girlfriend! We can't both be in the kitchen together because it's TOO SMALL! Where are you going to put the mattress? On the dining room table?? You can't! Because we don't have a dining room or a table!"

"Franklin, please! The mattress can stay on the porch. I'll figure something out by this weekend. I promise. I already brought my other things over".

"What? Where did you put them? You don't have a key!"

Krystal said "I was trying to open a window, and your neighbor came out and was so nice! He told me I could put them in his house till you got home."

Albert? You gave your things to Albert? Damn it, now he'll want to hang out because he'll think I owe him one! This is it. I've learned my lesson. Never again." But his outrage was weakening, and JJ could tell by the lack of concern on Krystal's face that they had played this scene out before.

They arrived at the duplex that Franklin rented with his girlfriend. JJ had been there for dinner once before the girlfriend moved in. It was a neat little place, but JJ had heard some stories about the neighbor. As they pulled up, he was sitting on the front step and jumped up when they pulled in.

"Hey Franklin, I met your sister today. Oh, there you are Krystal" he said as he saw her jump out of the back.

She said, "hi again!" with a coquettish smile, and it occurred to JJ that Franklin probably worried too much about Krystal. She had some pretty good survival skills and would always land on her feet.

Franklin walked to the back of the van and opened the door. Before he pulled the mattress out, Krystal said "Is there a way to hide this on the back porch?"

Franklin said "It will have to stay on the front. The back porch isn't big enough."

"Can we hide it somehow? Like with a tarp?"

Franklin stopped "why? Hide it from who?"

"Mike" Krystal said, again with her little girl voice.

Franklin looked at her for a long minute. "You said he kicked you out."

"He did" Krystal wouldn't look at Franklin.

"Then why would he be looking for the bed.?"

"Well, he probably will think I shouldn't have taken it."

Franklin was looking like he was rested enough to muster the rage again. "Krystal, whose bed is this?"

"Well, both of ours. But he has a good job. He can get another one. I don't make enough to buy another one." Her voice was petulant.

Franklin struggled to lower his voice. "Krystal, who paid for this bed?"

"He did, but I tipped the delivery man! So, I guess we both did." She said triumphantly.

Franklin's voice hissed "You just made me steal a bed? If this bed is worth more than 500 dollars that is a felony. And I transported stolen property in a company vehicle. Do you realize what we just did?" His voice was a whisper. Something about his face must have silenced Krystal, and without either of them speaking he pushed the mattress back into the van and got into the driver's seat. Krystal hurried to hop in as the van pulled away. Nothing was said as they sped back to the house, with Krystal once again bearing the weight of the world on her back, this time with a very sullen expression on her face.

The van was flying and before long, JJ saw a red flashing light bouncing off the rearview mirror. JJ could only see the back of Franklin's head, but he could recognize a defeated man when he saw one.

Krystal straightened up as much as possible and extended a delicate hand to the cop for a handshake, making her eyes big and giving him her most alluring smile. The cop reached past Franklin to shake her hand and softened just a bit in his tone. As Franklin looked through his wallet for his license, Krystal, in her little girl voice, tried to explain that Franklin was helping her out of a mess. As he listened and waited for the license the cop surveyed the scene in the van and tried to make sense of it. The young woman bent at the waist and holding on to the driver's seat, her back bent under the weight of a full-size mattress, the young man in a wheelchair looking placidly in front of him, the young driver looking exhausted and beaten down. He wasn't sure what to make of it all, but it sure looked like it would take a lot of paper-work to describe.

"Officer, as I explained, my brother is trying to help me out of a domestic situation and...," glanced down as something wet touched her sandaled foot.

"Oh my God!" Krystal screamed as she stared at the floor.

Franklin spun around to see what she was looking at and was confused by the liquid splashing around her feet, then understood and said,

"Damn, JJ, I forgot to empty your urine bag. It's overflowing!"

Franklin turned to the officers "Can I just clean him up? None of this is his fault. Please?"

The trooper hesitated. He looked at Krystal's horrified face, Franklin's dazed expression, and JJ's blank affect. He looked again at JJ. Was that a trace of a smile? The cop just shook his head "do what you have to do and go home under the speed limit. And get her in a seatbelt." He walked away glad none of this was his problem.

Franklin took off his sweatshirt and sopped up the puddle, put his sister back in the front seat, disconnected JJ's urine bag and emptied it in the woods, and then did his best to wedge the mattress so that it would not fall on JJ. No one spoke a word.

They continued on, a little slower, and pulled into the driveway. Mike's truck was there, and they could see him unloading it and taking supplies to the shed, set a little way from his house. Krystal took charge of the situation immediately,

"Pull around to the back and I'll distract him while you get the mattress in. The back door should still be open."

Krystal crossed in front of the van and walked towards the front of the house, out of JJ's sight. Franklin, who looked exhausted, pulled the mattress out and alternately carried and tugged it to the porch, up the stairs, and out of sight. JJ's heart was pumping. Krystal didn't seem scared when she walked by him. He thought the boyfriend was dangerous. What if he realized what she and Franklin had done? Would he become violent? Did he have a gun?

JJ was relieved when Franklin again appeared in front of the van. He climbed in and glanced at JJ and said "Never again JJ. Never again. I am going to be so straight after this if I manage to get through the night without losing my job."

He backed the van up and did an a-turn, scanning the yard nervously for Krystal. He wondered what excuse for being there she had given to Mike. "I don't know, JJ, should I go find her? What the hell is going on?" Just then, he saw her. Franklin said to JJ, "they look pretty friendly for two people who just broke up."

They came into JJ's view, their arms around each other's waists, with silly smiles on their faces.

"Franklin, I don't think you ever met Mike. Mike, this is my big brother. Mike and I broke up yesterday over a ridiculous argument and we just realized that it was nothing. He wants me to move back in. You probably don't have time to bring my things back from your house do you Franklin?"

Franklin started to chuckle. He sounded a bit like a crazy person, JJ thought, but who could blame him. "No, no time. Got to get JJ home. Good night. Nice to meet you Mike. Krystal, don't call me for a long, long time." Krystal frowned and Mike looked confused. JJ thought this was the best outing ever.

CHAPTER 22

The next day Franklin was out sick. He had warned JJ that he would probably not be in. He was exhausted and needed to spend some quality time with his girlfriend Brandi, who had found out about Krystal's plans to set up housekeeping with them and now needed a little reassurance that Franklin had his priorities in order.

Gina had been asked to cover his shift, and while she looked very tired, she smiled and gave JJ the quiet morning he needed after yesterday's excitement.

Gina announced JJ was going to take a bath. JJ was thrilled! Baths were few and far between! He got a shower every other night, strapped into a shower chair which was less comfortable than his wheelchair. But a bath. In an Argo tub. He would be strapped into a lift, and a flotation device placed under his arms, and he would be lowered into the warm deep-water soaking tub, gloriously weightless for an hour. The warmth and the hydro-jets would penetrate to his very bones. The bath gel would smell like grass after it was mowed, his head would be massaged as his hair was shampooed with an herbal smelling shampoo, he would lay back and savor every minute of it.

And Gina was the best for baths, next to Maria of course. She would be patient and not rush him. She may struggle to stay awake after working all night, but she would let him stay in the tub as long as policy allowed.

In a good month he would have two baths. April had included only one, so he was due.

He loved every minute of it. When he was finally lifted up out of the tub his skin was wrinkled, he glowed with improved circulation, and he was asleep before he was dressed.

He was sorry to have to get up for lunch. He was having a great pre-accident dream, involving a cute girl who had been in his science class in 8th grade. They had one date, which involved attending a school basketball game and a minute of passion under the bleachers. He woke up smiling and wondered what had become of her. She was his first kiss. He wished he could have another hour in bed, maybe relive it once again, but it was lunchtime.

After a leisurely, if unimpressive, meal, Gina took him for a brief walk, but she was exhausted and only made it halfway around the block. They sat in the back yard for a while, listening to the birds and feeling the soft breeze on their faces. Gina was squirming to stay awake, and JJ was relieved for her sake when his afternoon positioning time rolled around. After getting him back into bed, she was told to use her lunch break to take a quick nap, and not to worry if it went beyond 30 minute.

CHAPTER 23

JJ woke to see Gary back in his room. On his way in Gary had spotted Molly, so he was more attentive to Wayne than usual, expecting her to pop in at any minute. And she did.

"Mr. Whitestone, um Gary," Molly started. "I'm afraid we've seen no real improvement with the G-tube. It's only been a few days, but Wayne is really very weak. He had an episode of choking last night, and the dietician is recommending downgrading his diet to a ground, at least temporarily. We need to schedule an MRI for next week."

"What can you learn from that?" Gary asked, eyebrows knit together with apparent concern.

"Possibly any disease process or blockage that may explain the deterioration we're seeing. The doctor was hoping to avoid this because he's not sure Wayne will tolerate the procedure, but he feels we should try."

Gary thanked her and said he would sign any consent that was needed. He walked towards the bed and JJ heard him say to

Wayne. "Whatever will help my brother, right Wayne?" JJ seethed at the man's callous hypocrisy.

When Molly left and closed the door Gary punched some numbers into his phone and said, with no greeting. "We have to move pretty soon. They're doing more tests. I don't want them to get an MRI that shows no disease and then want to do an autopsy to figure out what happened when he dies. I think a few more days will be it. Got to keep him weak with the Tetrachloride and then one final dose.

He quietly busied himself at Wayne's side, JJ assumed injecting the poison. The door opened and Molly returned with the consent paperwork. Gary signed it and asked if the date could be the very end of next week, since he would be busy earlier in the week and he wanted to be able to accompany Wayne to the appointment. Molly said of course.

When she left, Gary gathered his things and looked up as he left to see JJ attentive and following his movement.

"Going to miss our daily visits, kid?", he said and laughed as he walked out the door. JJ was cold with a sense of dread. Gary seemed to be very interested in him lately, and JJ was pretty sure that was not a good thing.

CHAPTER 24

Gina took the better part of the afternoon to prepare JJ for the evening. Like Joe, she was kind and thorough but very slow. It was probably why they both ended up on the night shift.

As she was using the lift to position JJ back into his chair a woman who he had never seen before came into the room with Supervisor.

"Hi JJ, Gina," Supervisor said. "This is Debra Mullen. She works with the investigation unit. She is helping us work on a couple of recent incidents."

Ms. Mullen nodded and smiled at the two of them. She then asked if Gina wanted to take a quick break because they wouldn't need her for a few minutes. Gina, who was practically asleep on her feet, didn't mind at all.

When she left, Ms. Mullen asked supervisor to explain what kind of supports JJ needed and what appropriate positioning looked like. JJ had just been expertly positioned by Gina, which made this explanation much easier. Supervisor pointed out the trunk orthotic and explained how it supported his weight in an upright position from the hips up to his neck, keeping his organs aligned, his airway open, and making swallowing possible. She also explained the need to cinch the seatbelt tight over his hips to prevent his body from slipping down, and to keep his chair back at a 90-degree angle during meals as this prevented choking. She attested to the fact that all staff attended a four hour Therapeutic Feeding training before being allowed to assist anyone with eating, and that Jason had definitely been to the initial preservice training, the annual in-service refresher as recently as January, and had been trained specifically in JJ's safe dining plan as recently as last October.

Sweet, JJ thought, that whole choking thing was not a dead issue. Maybe they finally had enough to hang Jason.

Supervisor went on to explain the difference between what should have been, and what was, on the day of the incident. Ms. Mullen was listening with a very serious expression. Supervisor made a point describing Jason's demeanor upon finding out he was stuck on overtime. Ms. Mullen wanted to know, if Supervisor was aware of Jason's weakness as a staff, angry mood, and bad attitude, had she made a point of checking that his care that night was adequate. Supervisor seemed to take this as a rebuke and a bit defensively said not until she noticed JJ choking, because she was in the midst of audit preparation and was very busy. As she listened and took notes, Ms. Mullen glanced up at JJ several times. She seemed to look straight into his eyes. JJ wasn't used to this kind of attention.

Satisfied that she understood what the pertinent facts of the incident were, Ms. Mullen turned to the issue of the missing clothing.

JJ was surprised there was still interest in this since everything had ultimately materialized. "So, you checked everywhere and then it showed up where it should have been all along.?" "Yes, and I've talked to every staff and none of them found it and put it away. I'm mystified."

The investigator looked at the new clothing. JJ wondered if she thought they were old men's clothes, but probably that was not her concern.

"So, JJ, what do you think? Any idea who could have returned it?"

JJ froze. Rarely did anyone other than his closest staff ever look for information from him. He wished he knew, since it seemed to matter to all of them, but he wouldn't be able to express it if he did. But she waited for a minute, looking at him curiously. Supervisor didn't say anything right away, but after a minute or two she answered a bit timidly, "JJ isn't able to communicate for the most part. His closest staff can tell when he likes or agrees with something sometimes, but that's about it."

"I'm surprised they have not found a device for him yet. You look like you have things to say." She directed the latter to JJ, who was struck that an outsider who could see that inside his useless body, he was still thinking and having opinions.

He thought about that all evening, the strangeness of her wanting to hear what he had to say. He liked the idea.

After the accident, his life was a blur. He remembered very little of the crash and the immediate aftermath. His memory then was terrible. He couldn't remember what he ate for dinner five minutes after the meal was taken away. He couldn't move a muscle, couldn't turn his head, and while he could see images in front of him, his brain wouldn't translate them into useful information, so he would stare emotionless at his father, his friends, his doctor. They all believed that brain activity was gone.

After what seemed to be a long while, some improvement came, but not really in time. He was moved after a few months to a rehab center. The Physical Therapists, Occupational Therapists, Speech Therapists, Psychologists, all evaluated him, but found little to work with. He did not seem to have any volitional movement, and the occasional movement of his left hand was deemed a spasm. The Speech Therapist tried to harness his eye gaze for communication purposes, but his response time was so slow they found it unreliable.

Truthfully, he was emotionally not in a good place for showing what he could do. He was confused, his life had turned upside down. He was scared, he saw no chance of a decent life in his present shell of a body. And mostly he was angry, at himself, his father, and every other human being he saw. Angry that they hadn't saved him from himself, angry that they had lives, and he clearly no longer did.

He continued like that for a few weeks, after which he was deemed "not an appropriate candidate for Rehab." Without Medicaid paying the big bucks for Rehab, he was shuttled to the long-term units, where the people were biding their time until death. Truthfully, his care had been mostly kind, probably because of his young age, but life was pretty awful in that place. He was almost comatose with depression and boredom.

His Dad had visited the hospital, usually sober, in the early days. In Rehab, his visits were less frequent, maybe once or twice a week. In fairness to his Dad, JJ wasn't very good company. And when he went to the long-term unit, Dad came occasionally, usually drunk, and generally left with tears running down his face.

Dad had come to Cedar Hills, his present home, soon after JJ arrived. He was sober that day and dressed nicely. He seemed relieved and relaxed and told staff he thought JJ looked happier than he had in a while. JJ had been hopeful that this might be the beginning of a renewed relationship with him. He left smiling, but never came back. Who knew if he was still alive? JJ couldn't ask, and staff seemed to know it was a sensitive subject, because his Dad was rarely mentioned.

When JJ was able to be more dispassionate about it, though, he had to admit that his Dad may not realize it mattered to JJ. He would spend the whole visit looking straight ahead, not able to respond in any meaningful way to anything his Dad said. His Dad had never met Franklin or Maria. If he had visited when one of them were on, they might have been able to show him how to read the little signs that showed he was responsive. Without those signs, JJ looked oblivious to any attention he got from others.

JJ thought if he was ever given a chance to try again with a communication device, he would try harder to convince them he could do it. If they had left it with him and he could have practiced, he thought he might have gotten faster and more accurate. He realized now how important it was. At the time he was so angry, their efforts to help seemed woefully inadequate.

Now, while he certainly still would prefer to be the cocky 17-year-old who thought he was going to live forever, he had learned to love himself as he was. This transformation had occurred because of the people he met along the way who treated him like he was worth something. A nurse named Ceola who had since left the house but had been like a mother to him when he arrived, and a whole series of staff, most of whom had moved on, but who had made life livable during the time they spent with him. Now he was content to know that Franklin, Maria, and a few others could still see him, see his essence, and he clung to the value they placed on his life.

That night, when he was in bed, he practiced the skill he believed he would need to communicate with a device. He had seen a few. The fancy ones had pictures or letters you could touch or look at to communicate words. The simple ones were the words "Yes" or "no" that you only had to focus on. But he would have to do it quickly and consistently. He was going to practice so the next time he'd be ready, if he ever got a chance to be evaluated again.

CHAPTER 25

JJ's chance came earlier rather than later. He was in the dining room when a very harried Speech Therapist breezed in and said to Derrick, his staff for the day, "he hasn't finished eating yet has he? I need to evaluate him."

JJ actually had just started. For the next half an hour the woman managed to disrupt JJ's meal, watching him eat different foods, writing things down in her notebook, trying a few different textures, and finally pronouncing "He does fine with a regular diet. We'll leave him on that. Now, when he's done eating, I have to evaluate his communication before you put him down. I'll need to talk to you."

She hurried out to write her diet orders.

Supervisor rolled her eyes and said to Derrick, "The investigator pulled the Speech Eval and found out they're almost a year overdue, so she got her hand slapped. Hence, the attitude."

"OH" Derrick said, amused.

When they went into the bedroom, the Therapist asked Derrick if he was able to communicate with JJ. He said he and others could generally tell if JJ liked something or not, but she should speak to Franklin and Maria, they seemed to be able to communicate with him the best.

She dismissed the idea, "I checked when they are in and I can't wait that long. The eval has to be in by the weekend."

She gave a few commands "Look here, look there" but didn't wait long enough for a response.

"His last five evals all say he is able to smile minimally and that is his best communication behavior. Would you agree?" She obviously did not care whether Derrick agreed or not.

"I guess," he shrugged and looked helplessly at JJ.

The therapist mumbled thank you without looking at either of them and left.

JJ was disappointed. He guessed that was his chance, and now he'd have to wait another year.

CHAPTER 26

It was close to 4 and JJ was waiting for Maria to get there. She was back and he couldn't wait to see her.

For the last hour he had been awake and practicing his communication skills. He would decide what he wanted to say, then search his calendar, which hung below the clock positioned across from the bed, and find the letters or numbers, staring at each for a second before moving on to the next one. He was extremely slow, but he thought he might be picking up speed. He wished he had an alphabet in front of him so he would have more letters to work with.

He imagined being asked a question and answering it using his gaze. "JJ, what do you want for dessert?" P....i..... he knew pie was spelled with an e but there wasn't an e in sight. And he definitely would not pick pie over ice cream or cake, but the calendar was still set on April even though it was already May 4th, so he had to work with the letters he could find.

"JJ how old are you?" ...2...7..

For two more days he thought.

Maria came in smiling at 4:15. She affirmed that Brad was in jail and said that was the last she intended to mention his name. Today was about having a nice day.

JJ's good day was ruined when minutes later he heard the caustic sound of Jason's voice. Maria noticed JJ stiffen when he heard Jason boasting to Valerie, and she patted his hand.

"Yes, Cariño I know he is back but don't worry. Mona said she will never make him your staff again. She promised. And don't worry, he was punished."

During dinner Jason stayed away from JJ's table and swaggered like he was just back from vacation, not a two-week suspension for neglect. JJ was ready to glare at him if there was an opportunity, but Jason avoided eye contact completely.

During dinner the conversation turned to investigations. Valerie and Jason talked about the determination of neglect and some penalties that resulted in his return to work, in euphemisms of course, as if JJ didn't know what they were talking about. Maria ignored them and tried to keep JJ distracted, but he hung on every word. Sounded like Jason got his hand slapped pretty good, he thought. Good. Though after 20 minutes of discussion Jason ended it with "this job sucks, I was almost hoping I'd get fired." Valerie seemed to be trying to stay on Jason's good side but was clearly uncomfortable. He was an intimidating presence in the room.

When she could change the subject Valerie asked Maria if she had heard whether the missing clothing investigation was over. Maria said no she hadn't heard; she had just returned and had not caught up with the gossip yet. Jason's ears perked up and he asked for details. Valerie gave him the sequence of events, the clothes were bought one day, missing two days later, and mysteriously returned the following day. Jason lost interest when he realized it was not a very salacious crime. He shrugged and said "big deal. It happened before."

"Really? When?" Maria put her distain for Jason aside for a second because this was news to her which Mona might want to know about.

"Yeah, about six months ago someone bought a winter coat for Miriam and it was gone the next day. A couple of days later Gina found it in her closet. I don't think anyone ever told Mona."

JJ was not interested in the clothing or Miriam's coat, so he went back to concentrating on his hamburger and green beans. He glanced at Wayne, who was looking worse than ever, and not enjoying his ground hamburger. JJ felt bad for him, and helpless.

After dinner there was a short walk and then Maria gave him a manicure. As she clipped his nails and chattered, he longed to really talk to her today, not just listen to her. It had been a long time since he had really felt the need to share his thoughts, not to ask for something or say no to something or answer questions, but to really talk. He wished he could tell Maria about his outing with Franklin. He wasn't sure whether she would be horrified or would laugh at the whole incident. He needed to tell her about the poison that Gary was pumping into Wayne, making him weaker and weaker. He'd like to tell her he wanted a fish for his birthday, but then felt ridiculous for even thinking about such a silly thing in light of recent events.

But he was a patient man, and now that he had formulated a plan for long term use of some kind of device, he would practice using his eyes so that he was ready when the time came. In the meantime, he just listened to Maria carrying on a conversation about all the good things planned for his birthday, including a birthday cake, a special dinner, and (Maria winked) a gift he would not be expecting.

Franklin was in the next morning, with a bag of clothes from Target. JJ was curious- he wasn't that into clothes anymore, but sometimes Franklin managed to bring back the cool factor in his wardrobe. High School had been about envying the kids with the name brands and newest sneakers. Nothing like losing control of your body to make you realize how meaningless it all was.

Franklin threw the bag on the bed and said "I hope you like what I got J. I told Mona next time I'm taking you. You could pick out what you like. I figured this time I better get rid of those old man clothes or you'd be ruining your swagger, ya know what I mean?"

He pulled the clothing out and showed them to JJ. Some Nike sports shirts ("got 'em on sale J") A couple of tee shirts with classic bands like Springsteen and ACDC ("Classic's in, bro") And some athletic shorts. Much better JJ thought. When Mona came to see what he'd brought back she made a face, but she let it be.

"Weird thing though, Mona," Franklin said, as he packed everything up for washing and labeling, "The dude at Customer

Service said the stuff was returned once already and repurchased according to their records.

"That is odd," Mona shook her head. This whole thing made no sense.

Franklin was administering medications this day, so JJ ate a little later than usual. He sat at the table trying to find something with letters in his field of vision, but there were no posters, or emails, reminders, nothing. He tried to use words on the TV, but the screen changed too fast. He gave up when breakfast arrived.

After breakfast they sat in the yard for a while. While Franklin worked in the garden and talked his way through this year's plantings, JJ's mind drifted to Wayne and his brother. Was the man seriously going to take out his brother to cash in on his mother's death? That was like a plot to movie. How could JJ possibly intervene?

JJ didn't quite understand what medication Gary was giving Wayne. Tetra-something-or -other. Gary seemed to be taking his time. Apparently the last six months of visits with recent poisoning was meant to take the focus off Gary when Wayne finally died. If he had done it right away there might have been suspicion cast his way. How does a person do that? JJ had been angry enough with someone to land a punch when he was younger, but to slowly poison someone you were related to, watching them get sicker and sicker, knowing you were going to finish them off? That was cold, man.

After a bit of planting Franklin announced they needed to rest their butts and he needed to rest his back. He brought the guys back in and gave each a quick snack then back to the room for a rest. Wayne was first, and JJ waited patiently, hoping Franklin would hang out a bit after putting him down and keep him company. He wanted Franklin to drill him with choices like he had the other night. It was great training for his long-term goal of getting his hands on a device, figuratively speaking.

Franklin must have been reading his mind, because as he turned to help JJ, he began to "demand" answers.

"So, you want the tv on?" Franklin asked, after lowering him to the bed. He waited till JJ rolled his eyes distinctly to the right. Franklin beamed, proud of himself and JJ. JJ actually felt somewhat empowered with just that simple ability to say "Yes".

Franklin teased him by tuning the tv to Days of Our Lives. "Is this what you want to watch?" He asked with a grin. JJ glared straight ahead.

"How about this?" He flipped a channel and showed him Discovery Channel for a minute. JJ thought for a second and decided to pass.

"No? What about this?" It was a Skateboard championship of some kind. JJ rolled his eyes to the right. Might be worth a half hour of his time.

Franklin sat next to the bed and watched for a few minutes before he got bored. He apologized to JJ about the nonsense with his sister the other night, and began to recount it, laughing at the ridiculous sight they must have made. JJ smirked also-it really was funny in retrospect. Actually, JJ had thought it was funny that night, but he could understand why Franklin wouldn't think so. He was glad to hear Franklin's girlfriend had forgiven him for almost letting Krystal move in with them. Franklin thought he probably should break down and start taking Krystal's calls again. She was, after all, his sister. After a bit Franklin left for a break.

Wayne's brother was in at 11:30, earlier than usual. He was talking to his accomplice on the phone.

"I just got a new bottle. I'm not sure what a lethal dose is... I'll up the dose faster from this point on. He doesn't look like he's in pain, he looks weak...I know, I'm not trying to torture him, but I don't want them to be suspicious when it happens. Another day or two at the most, then Mother will pass from cancer, and this whole thing will be over, and I can start enjoying lunch again."

The door opened and he hung up the phone quickly, and Franklin came in with the med cart. He was finishing charting Miriam's meds, then and then broke the insulin syringe's needle off in the sharps container and tossed the syringe in the small trash receptacle on top of the med cart. Franklin went to the bathroom to wash his hands, then applied the topical cream to JJ's hands before lunch, which Franklin took care of in silence, not wanting to talk to JJ with Gary there.

In the hall JJ heard Mona call, "Can I take Miriam out to the dining room? Did you give her her insulin?"

"Yeah, just finished it." Franklin called out. He finished his documentation and left with the cart.

Gary called his brother back, "Sorry to cut you off, someone came in. But I just figured out how we're going to make this foolproof."

At lunch Franklin made a point of asking for a yes from JJ for everything he could think of, probably to show off.

"Do you want coffee with your meal J?" He knew he did.

"Do you want me to give you your sandwich first?" JJ didn't care but said yes anyway.

"Is the soup hot enough, J?" Enough already, JJ thought. But it was having the desired effect. Derrick, Julie, and Supervisor all thought it showed just how smart JJ was, which they of course suspected all along. JJ found that amusing.

"I wish you were here when the speech lady came and evaluated him. She didn't give him a chance. I told her he's slow to answer but if you watch his face you can tell, and she didn't take the time." Derrick said to Franklin.

Next time I'll be ready, JJ thought.

He knew what kind of communication device he wanted because he had seen a number of them over the years. Sometimes a motivated therapist would bring a couple to try out, always concluding he lacked a consistent response to make them worthwhile. But the one he had seen which was perfect was actually used by a guy named Matthew. He had only been at the house for a few months before he won a big lawsuit and got a ton of money for the accident that left him disabled, and he then moved into his own apartment with round the clock care.

JJ liked to think they were a lot alike. Matthew had been driving a car when a tractor trailer crossed the line and hit him head on. The driver had fallen asleep. Matthew was a quadriplegic and needed supports similar to JJ, but in addition he wore a halo to support his head and had a difficult time with eating.

The communication device was a wonder. With it, Matthew could control so many things in his life, including how people viewed him. He had pre-programmed the device to have responses ready for many situations. If Franklin had asked him "Do you want coffee, the answer wouldn't have been "yes", it would have been "yes, please, light cream and two sugars." He had pre-programmed some angry responses for those times he was not being treated well, though they made him delete the one that said "F..You!" He could use his eye gaze to spell out many words and phrases, but he was slow like JJ, so he would often write lengthy responses while the person who questioned him would busy themselves taking care of others or doing clean up, then come back to hear his answer. JJ admired him and envied him more than he had anyone else since he'd been hurt. Matthew left a few years ago, and JJ often wondered how much he would have learned from Matthew if he had stayed. Matthew was his own man. JJ was too, but only a few people knew it.

The device was marvelous. If JJ had ever known during his rehabilitation that such a thing existed, he would have handled the therapy evaluations very differently. Now it seemed he was going to have an uphill battle to get someone to take his potential seriously since they were guided by earlier reports. But he had learned patience above all things since his injury, and next year hopefully he would have another chance.

After lunch they went for a quick walk around the block, then back to bed for repositioning. JJ got really tired of it, but he knew his skin was fragile and if they didn't get him off his buttocks regularly, he would end up with a breakdown, and possibly endure the indignity that poor Mike had been subjected to a few weeks ago. He had developed a pressure area after his wild day with Franklin a couple of days ago, but one day of side positioning seems to have helped, because they didn't see the need today. JJ was disappointed- he would have liked a day to watch Gary.

Maria had told JJ yesterday that she would not be in tonight but would be back for his birthday tomorrow. She had to go collect her things from her old apartment with Brad, and the court had ordered a police escort to do so. She told him she thought Joe would take her place, and to be nice to him. JJ was over the whole Joe thing-they were fine.

But come 4:15 Valerie came in, not Joe. She explained that Joe would be a little late. She was not her usual sassy self, J thought. She moved slowly, her mind elsewhere, and mascara smeared below her eyes seemed to indicate she had been crying.

Valerie had never been assigned to him before, possibly because Supervisor, at some level, understood that it could be embarrassing for J. He actually wished she hadn't been assigned, because he didn't want her involved with his intimate care. But as she went about her work, he had to admit she was professional and competent. In fact, she reminded him a bit of Maria.

When Joe came in at around 4:45 he also noticed Valerie was upset. He thought she was mad at him for being late and apologized.

"No problem at all." She seemed surprised that he would think she cared about his punctuality.

She was pleasant to JJ and to Joe, but her lip trembled, and she seemed to be barely holding it together.

Joe closed the door and asked what was wrong. She shook her head, "nothing", but then sat down in the visitor's chair and tears flowed. Joe handed her a tissue and looked like he would have liked to be anywhere but where he was. Finally, after getting her composure back, she told him she had been asked to meet with Supervisor for her Performance Evaluation. She really thought it was going to be a good. She thought everyone liked her. She thought she did a good job, she loved working here. She never called in, was always on time.

But Mona had told her she seemed immature, the job demanded a great deal of professionalism, and Mona didn't feel confident that she understood that. Valerie had asked for one instance where she had not provided good supportive care to the people she was assigned to, but Mona only talked about the impressions she made, about being flirtatious with staff and the people who lived there, a preoccupation with her looks, etc. Valerie vented to Joe, who was very sorry he had asked, that while she admitted those things may be true to some extent, she also did a damn good job that no one noticed. She was much better than Jason, and he still worked there! She had been put on probation.

If she did not improve in the next ten days she would be let go. And with that the tears flowed again. "I love this job!" she cried. " I love these people." She said as she grabbed J's hand and squeezed. JJ felt so bad for her he wished he could squeeze it back.

Joe did his best to console her, but he really didn't know what to say. They went to the dining room for dinner and Valerie was very quiet the rest of the evening. When she was in his line of sight, JJ watched her work with new eyes. She was very good. She was careful with positioning, she talked to her people respectfully, she fed them carefully. Maybe he had been wrong about her-she didn't look like an airhead at all. He and at least some of the men of the house had seen her as a pretty young thing, never realizing she was more than that. He felt a little guilty. He could feel his mother's disapproval and vowed to do better.

After dinner they watched Jeopardy again, and when the champion was finally deposed after weeks of dominance there were mixed feelings in the room. They hung out for the rest of the evening. Joe was not the social animal Franklin was, but he sat between Wayne and JJ and carried on with as much banter as he could think of and when he ran out, they sat in a comfortable silence.

Tomorrow was JJ's birthday. 28 years old. Not going to be a wild party or anything, but he would have his favorite meal, or at least what Maria thought was his favorite meal. He wished he could tell her it was steak, not lasagna, but that was alright. Lasagna was good too.

His mom always made steak for his birthday and his Dad's. Filet Mignon, she would announce formally, "Tonight we eat like kings." She always decorated the table and made a show of serving it. Presents would come after, usually what he'd asked for or as close to it as they could afford. He didn't remember ever being disappointed.

After his mother died, Dad's work dried up because his drinking got out of control. He was a contractor when he was first married, lost the business in the recession and became a carpenter for another contractor, and after his wife's death and an uptake in drinking, which culminated in being caught drinking on the job, was fired. Last JJ knew he was a handyman, with a handful of customers who hired him out of pity or because he worked cheap.

JJ used to remind him of his birthday ahead of time, less because he expected any celebration and more because his father needed to know how old he was for different forms he would have to fill out. He usually managed a card, maybe with a five in it, but not every year.

Bedtime was about nine, though Cedar Hill was pretty chill about it, maybe because it was better staffed than some places. In Rehab and at the Long-Term Care facility JJ had been put to bed for the night at seven. It made for an endless night and had caused JJ to become quite depressed. When he lived at home, he had gone to bed between 11 and 12, but now he didn't mind nine- it gave him a little while to contemplate his day before falling asleep.

JJ waited while Wayne was showered and in bed, then got a quick shower and into bed himself. Joe tidied up the room and picked up some department store bags from the foot of Wayne's bed.

Joe pulled out some shirts and shorts and held them up for JJ to see. JJ smirked; Mona must have shopped. Joe hung them up in the closet-they would have to be tried on, then washed and labeled before he would wear them.

JJ slept well that night, only waking up once to hear Wayne's wardrobe door opening and closing. He assumed Joe or Gina were putting away laundry.

CHAPTER 27

JJ's birthday came and he greeted it with good humor and low expectations. Franklin came in singing a version of Happy Birthday with lyrics that included some adult content. He made eggs and bacon for breakfast. Then a walk in the neighborhood, a long visit with the dog, and back to the house for a quick snack. JJ was a bit annoyed when as soon as the 30 minute-after meals-upright- order was reached, Franklin ushered him off to bed for repositioning.

Franklin could tell J was mad and he laughed "don't get your knickers in a knot, bro, you're going to be down for the minimum of an hour and then we got things to do."

JJ thought Franklin had something up his sleeve. He stared at the calendar practicing his response time for the hour: "J, do you want syrup on your pancakes?" "Yes please" he typed with his eyes. "JJ do you want Jason to drop dead?" "Yes please".

As promised in exactly one-hour Franklin appeared and announced that Mona gave him permission to take JJ to the matinee that started at 1:00. JJ was thrilled- Franklin always made good on his promises. He ate a quick early lunch and they hit the road.

The movie was great. Liam Nielson played a secret service agent trying to save the president from a series of ridiculous attacks. Franklin let him have a few pieces of popcorn but was nervous about it because popcorn is such a choking hazard, so he cut him off and switched to the large box of Reese's Pieces. He got a coke. The dietician would have a stroke if she saw him.

They got home at 3:30 and JJ was more than willing to take a break in bed before dinner. Maria was already there and had greeted him with a balloon bouquet which she brought to his room. She was assigned to meds, and after leaving Miriam's room, rolled the med cart into JJ's room. JJ saw Gary lurking in the hall, but he didn't follow her in, instead watching her document Miriam's insulin and dispose of the syringe.

When she went to the bathroom to wash her hands, and chattered at JJ all the while, Gary appeared from the hall, strode to the cart and quickly, with a gloved hand, scooped the syringe from the trash before Maria reappeared in the room. When she stepped out of the bathroom, he startled her, and they stared at each other for a minute before she gave him a cool smile, finished up with JJ's topical treatment, then left with the cart. JJ wasn't entirely sure what Gary had in mind, but he was sure it wasn't good for Maria.

Supervisor popped her head in and said "Good afternoon Mr. Whitestone. Just wanted to check in." She had done that a few times since the open G-tube incident.

They exchanged pleasantries and, on her way out, she said " I thought you would want to know we picked up some new clothes for Wayne. They're in his closet if you want to see them. "

Gary could care less, but he wanted to be sure to have Mona in his corner should there be any questions after Wayne's death. "Do you have a minute to show me?" he asked.

Mona, as he suspected, was pleased to be asked. She opened the doors to his closet and looked, then his dresser, then excused herself and went to the laundry room. She came back with a tight smile and said "In the wash! I'll show you tomorrow."

That evening while Maria and the other staff tried to make dinner and the single slice of birthday cake festive, Mona searched every corner of the house for Wayne's new clothes. She returned to sing to JJ, but he could tell she was not happy.

After dinner, the candle was blown out and a couple of presents were given to JJ. Valerie presented the first: some new men's cologne, some funky socks, and a pair of sunglasses that JJ was surprised he actually liked. Maria gave him a gift and whispered in his ear "from me, because we are special friends". JJ knew staff were discouraged from giving gifts to prevent hurt feelings in the event anyone was left out. The gift was a fishbowl with a beautiful blue Chinese fighting fish. JJ curled his lip in appreciation. Somehow, she always knew.

After he was in bed for the night and the fish was positioned on an over-the-bed table so he could see it, Maria sat down on the bed and said

"JJ, I didn't want to give you this earlier because I wasn't sure how you would feel about it. She took out an envelope and pointed to the return address, "it's from your father."

JJ shut his eyes for a moment. This was the first contact his father had made in several years.

" Do you want me to open it?"

JJ looked to the right. Maria opened the envelope and some photos fell on the bed. She read the card, which was a simple birthday message "I think about you often. I hope you are happy and don't hate me too much. I'm sorry I let you down." Love Dad Tears of anger brimmed in his eyes and distorted his vision. Maria was quiet and let him have a moment. Then she picked up the three photos on the bed and looked at them, smiled, and turned them around for him to see. They were pictures of a lovely tall woman and a dark-haired boy around 8 years old. He and his Mom at the beach.

CHAPTER 28

The next morning was Franklin's day off again. Derrick was assigned to JJ and they had a quiet pleasant morning. Around 10, before morning re-positioning, Debra Mullen was back, this time with another woman. They spoke to Supervisor near the office door, then headed over to JJ.

Debra said to JJ "I hope you remember me James. We spoke last week. I had asked the speech therapist to come see you, and she did an evaluation, but your staff think she may have underestimated your ability to communicate. Do you agree with them?" JJ looked to the right. Derrick excitedly told her "Franklin taught him to do that! It means yes. We used to watch to see if he smiled or not, but this is better."

"I bet it is." She said addressing both JJ and Derrick. "I asked my friend Ann here to come and see if she could do another more in-depth evaluation, because the other therapist felt pressed for time. James, this is Ann Flores, Ann this is James Johnson." He tried to give her his best smile. He didn't want to get his hopes up, but this could be huge.

Ann spent most of the morning with JJ. When she realized he spent hours in bed because of the need to prevent breakdown she asked if she could do the evaluation in his room. Wayne was asleep, but Derrick assured her that he would not be disturbed if she worked with JJ. Derrick was excited for JJ, to the point where Ann finally sent him on an errand so she could better assess JJ's skills without distraction

What she found was considerably different than what his past evals had shown. There was clear intention and desire to communicate. He was able to blink consistently, but since blinking was also involuntary, she explained it wasn't the best motor response for communication. She was able to see his finger movement and the arm movement, but it took so much effort and so much time she felt that was not a useful avenue to pursue. The gaze though was consistent, didn't seem to fatigue him, and was efficient. His lack of head movement would present some problems. The device would have to allow for a number of choices within a small area. She was not sure yet whether he would be able to "turn" virtual pages to access more choices. She did not try letter selection, but decided JJ was a good candidate for therapy and was sure that a device which would give him back his voice could be found. JJ was exhilarated, and Derrick only a little less so. He summoned Supervisor to JJ's room to hear what the plans were.

As Ann apprised Supervisor and Derrick of her plans for further evaluation and gave them some ideas as to how they could maximize JJ's expressive language in the meantime, JJ noticed Gary lurking at the door. After a couple of minutes, he entered the room, nodding at the group, and the discussion of JJ's treatment was ceased due to privacy needs. Ann thanked JJ and Derrick for their cooperation and assured him, with a wink, they would be spending a lot of time together.

Derrick walked Ann out and told JJ he'd be back in a minute to get him up. They left and shut the door, and while Gary was not in JJ's direct sight, he could feel his eyes boring through him. JJ heard him completing his daily dosing of Wayne, then his face, full of menace, appeared at the foot of JJ's bed.

"Well, we're going to have to figure out how to handle this new wrinkle won't we? My gut told me you were trouble a while ago." He glared for a minute, then left.

CHAPTER 29

The evening was a bit tense because once again, a theft had taken place. Valerie was convinced they would think it was her because she was new, but Maria reminded her that Miriam's coat was taken and then brought back before Valerie was hired. Jason thought it was a set-up, he knew Mona didn't like him and would love a reason to can him. JJ was sure the last part of that suspicion was right. Maria wondered aloud why someone would go through the trouble of taking things just to bring them back?

Supervisor was taking this all very personally. She was the most respected House Manager in the agency, and this was making her look bad. JJ was aware through gossip that she was up for a promotion to Assistant Director of Residential Services. These thefts were not what she needed right now.

Valerie was a different person today. She was pleasant but not buoyant, and she was dressed in a simple button up shirt with a pair of loose-fitting khaki pants that hid all of the curves that JJ loved so well. She was apparently determined to give Mona no excuse to let her go.

After dinner Maria took JJ for a walk around the block. She told him as they walked that she was very relieved to be able to walk without worrying about Brad showing up, but that her lawyer had warned her that there was a chance he would get bail at his hearing. JJ was shocked that this was a possibility. She said if he was released, she would have to be very careful until the trial.

JJ thought he knew what she must be feeling before, but today it was a visceral understanding. He kept replaying Gary's cold menacing face at the end of his bed and his threatening message, and the residue of fear it left was as paralyzing as his injured spine.

They then turned to a lighter subject: "the new Chinese Fighting fish, or Siamese Fighting Fish, as she was told by the pet store, could live for 3-5 years. They are also called the Betta fish. They are very territorial, and the males especially are very aggressive. They can live with some other fish that are compatible..." At some point JJ thought she sounded a little like: "The Robin, also known as Robin Red Breast..."

That night, before she left him for the night, Maria taped up the pictures of his Mom and him at the beach on his over-the-bed table. "I'll pick up a frame for these soon JJ. Sleep tight."

JJ knew that was not likely.

CHAPTER 30

After breakfast the next day, JJ was surprised to see Ann again, and Debra Mullen was at her side. Ann said she was working on a device for him and Debra said she just needed to ask a few questions and hoped Ann could help JJ answer them. They went back to the room and the two women sat in the side chairs. Derrick was given time to do whatever he needed to do; they'd call him if they needed anything.

Debra started by asking JJ if he knew that clothing has been disappearing in the house. Ann told him to use his "look to the right" eye gaze to say yes and asked him to look to the left to say "no". She held up two cards that had the words and symbols on them. He looked right. She asked him if he was aware, they were returned, and he looked right. She asked him if he knew who had taken them and he looked left. She asked him if he knew who had returned them and he hesitated. It had occurred to him that Gina had been in the room the night before his clothes and Wayne's had been returned, and that she had been the one to find Miriam's coat. But he wasn't sure- he rolled his eyes to the right then the left.

Ann hesitated, then said "I'm not sure what that means. He is generally very decisive."

Debra looked like she wanted to pursue this but dropped it. "Thank you, JJ. Now I have questions about something else you may be able to help with. Do you remember the day Maria was attacked?"

JJ looked hard to the right.

Do you know who attacked her?"

Right again.

"Is it this man?"

She held a picture of Brad up and he again looked right.

"Is this the man? " she held up a picture of a man who resembled Brad but was not Brad.

JJ's eyes turned left. Ann and Debra looked at each other, seemingly satisfied.

"JJ, Maria's lawyers think it may help Maria if you were to go to court and tell them what you saw. They asked Ann and I if we thought you would be able to do this, and we believe you can. Do you think you can?"

JJ was floored. Him in court? Would they really believe him? Why wouldn't they believe Maria? But, of course, if it would help, he would try. With the slightest of hesitation, he looked right.

CHAPTER 31

These events pushed JJ's long delayed speech therapy into hyper drive. Ann soon introduced a variety of devices, all with the central feature of being eye gaze activated and gave JJ a chance to show his stuff. His practice on the calendar was paying off. He could give yes/no answers quickly, and she introduced "I don't know" and "maybe." She did alphabet testing with him and while he was still not smooth with his ability to scan and choose, she could tell that spelling with a device would be possible at some point in the future. She did some minimal sight word testing and he aced it, though his speed was still so slow that it was not feasible for natural communication.

She finally settled, after asking J's approval, on a device very similar to Matthew's device. It had the right sensitivity for his eye gaze ability. Few false starts, but not overly difficult to trigger. It could store common phrases and words so that conversation and responses required only one gaze at an icon, facilitating ease of communication. Ultimately if JJ learned to spell more efficiently, he could communicate more nuanced ideas and concerns by spelling them out, then storing them to be used when a listener was available.

JJ was excited beyond belief. His lip curled into a smile that wouldn't fade, making it no longer useful for communication because it was his constant expression. He envisioned a future that was full of freedom and control. Ann had no idea where he intended to take this- she had not yet realized who she was dealing with.

Then the devastating news: It could take up to 6 months to get approved through Medicaid. JJ's heart sank. He needed it now, no later than this week. He needed to tell someone about Gary before it was too late, for Wayne and maybe for himself.

He had a restless night thinking about what he could do. Maria was back tomorrow night. Maybe if he could show her, he was concerned about something she would help him tell Ann he needed a device now. But it was a long shot. Maria could sometimes read his mind, but he doubted she could divine that his look of concern had to do with impending murder.

But that afternoon his luck turned again. Ann was able to borrow one which was being unsuccessfully used with someone else. The other person's Speech Therapist was about to switch him to a less demanding device because her student hadn't been making progress, and Ann was able to have it right away. It was a device that had been used by someone who used to live at the agency but had donated it when he became financially independent and was able to buy a fancier model.

When she took it out of the case JJ recognized it right away-it was Matthew's old device, which JJ had dreamed of for years.

Ann was explaining that this device was not the latest model but was very similar to the one they had tried out, which had been on loan from the company. She had approached the company for a loaner or a rental, but the device was an $8,000-dollar machine, and the salesman's supervisor gave her a hard "no." They would have to wait for Medicaid to get a new one, but this one should help him get started.

Matthew's old device still had many of the preset phrases from when he had used it. It looked like a tablet, and when opened the home page had what Ann had set up, three options she wanted to begin with: Yes, No, I don't know. The words were in squares, with an accompanying icon. She explained to JJ and staff that these three expressions would give him some ability to make choices day to day, and also, if he became efficient, would allow him to testify in court.

The second page which was accessed by looking at a tab, gave him the alphabet screen. This was the Holy Grail. With this everything was possible. Ann told staff and JJ that he would start to work on spelling out words and "we'll see where it goes. It's a higher-level skill. I know that JJ has command of the alphabet, so it's kind of up to him if he wants to put the effort out or would rather add icons to the first page. It will depend also on what and how much he wants to communicate". She showed them how a word or phrase, once saved, could be accessed on the third page any time he wanted it. The three pages should allow for nearly full expressive ability.

The third page contained many of Matthew's old phrases. Don't worry about these for now, Ann said. Some of them may be useful and we will go through them one by one and you can decide which, if any you wanted to keep. JJ noticed one with the tag "FU" and smirked. Maybe Matthew hadn't gotten rid of it after all. JJ would use it at least once on Jason before they took it away.

The last thing was to pick a voice that JJ felt comfortable with, since it was speaking for him. The voice sounded electronic, but there were choices of age, race, and gender, with several choices in each category. He chose a voice that he thought sounded like a young white guy. When he got better at it, he thought he would have some fun with it and sound like Morgan Freeman or add an English accent, but now was not the time.

While JJ totally understood the process for using the board, and knew he had the skills necessary, actually doing so was more difficult than he had imagined. The process of finding the letters was not the difficult part-he had learned keyboarding skills as a child, so he recognized the Qwerty keyboard and quickly remembered the location of letters. The problem was moving his eyes quickly enough to avoid triggering letters.

It would come with practice, but time was short. And until a holder for it could be devised, his practice time was limited to a short time every day. On day one, he only managed to write the first two letters of the word that he hoped would save Wayne's life-URGENT. He typed u-r before he was told "enough for the day." and the machine was taken away. It was put in the office for charging. Staff had a protocol that he could use it in half hour increments until Ann gave them the go ahead, and a holder for it could be devised. But If he could finish the word, he was sure someone would sit with him and let him tell them what was so urgent.

CHAPTER 32

That evening Maria was almost as excited as JJ to learn about his communication device. She fired it up and held it where JJ could see it and began to ask him questions. "Do you want coffee with your meal?" She giggled to hear his machine voice say "Yes" "Do you know what the winning lottery numbers are?" Maria was amused and laughed with Valerie when JJ answered, "I don't know."

JJ would normally have played the game for a while, but he needed to get his message typed. He switched to page two, opened the file that contained "u-r" and added a "g", saving it before Maria said, "sorry JJ, Ann asked that I not let you use this page till she can work with you. Be patient and you will be using it all you want very soon. I have a feeling no one else will get a word in once you start!"

The smirk on JJ's face faded. He was so close to being able to warn them about Gary, but if he didn't get his message out in time close wouldn't be good enough. Since Gary's appearance by his bed JJ was skittish, reacting to every slight bump of his chair, or unexpected opening of a door.

After dinner Maria, JJ, Wayne, and Valerie took a walk. It was pleasant and JJ tried to relax and listened to the chatter of Maria and Valerie, who was quickly becoming "one of the gang". Valerie had toned down her wardrobe, stopped tousling his hair, and became very professional. JJ was quite disappointed.

As they walked, JJ saw a car parked across the street with a man behind the wheel. The man seemed to be watching them in his rear-view mirror, but as they passed the car JJ felt, rather than saw, eyes following him. A minute later the same car passed them, but when they turned the corner, he found it parked across the street further down the block, again watching them in the rear-view mirror. JJ recognized it as a Ford Focus, silver, older model. The man looked a bit familiar, but JJ couldn't place him from this distance. JJ felt eyes on the back of his head as they walked past the car. JJ's body stiffened even more than usual with fear. Was this the brother on the other end of the phone? The car was a beater, not the Mercedes Gary was known to drive. Did it have something to do with Brad? Geeze, JJ thought. Gary is making me paranoid.

That evening JJ felt a difference in the way he was regarded by others. Even Miriam spoke to him a couple of times, not ex-pecting an answer, but as if she expected him to understand her. Valerie was more careful in how she spoke in his presence- careful to address him directly, not speak to him through Maria. And Maria beamed like a proud mother. Or at least a proud older sister. JJ actually felt a bit overwhelmed at the thought that his relationships were about to change and wondered how he was going to handle it.

CHAPTER 33

During the night JJ woke to hear the door open. It made him jump, even though the door opened every thirty minutes every night. He heard someone rustling in Wayne's closet putting things away, which was surprising, because laundry was supposed to be put away at the end of the evening. While it wasn't unheard of for evenings to get behind and need the night staff to pick up the slack, it wasn't common. He waited for the closet door to shut and to see who stepped into the rectangle of light from the hallway on the way out of the room. He knew before he saw her it would be Gina.

As she closed the door Gina looked up and saw JJ looking at her. She looked startled but smiled and left quietly.

JJ lay in bed thinking. He had known in his heart for a while that the clothing was being taken and returned by Gina. He didn't get it- first because she would be just about the last person he would suspect of theft, and second because clearly, she didn't understand thievery didn't include returning the stolen items. He resolved to ask her to explain herself if he got the chance after he mastered his communication device.

140

But he didn't have to wait. About a half hour later the door cracked open and a sliver of light lit up a very worried looking Gina. She looked at JJ, realized he was still awake, and came to sit on the side of the bed. For a minute she said nothing but patted his hand. He rolled his eyes and looked at her usually cheerful face but saw only lines of worry.

"JJ, I'm not sure how much you understand, but I'm told by Maria and others that you are very smart. I can see in your eyes that you know what I have been up to, and I feel like I owe you an explanation. Maybe more like a confession. I know that you saw me the day I returned your clothing and I think you can guess that I was in here tonight returning Wayne's new clothing. The truth is I did take the clothing both times and I returned it a few days later. Last year I did the same thing with a new coat that Miriam had received. I am very ashamed but let me tell you why.

My husband is a maintenance man for a big Office building in the city. He takes a bus to work, and he works from 2 in the afternoon until 10:00 in evening. I have to be here by 11 o'clock and I also have to take a bus. When everything works well, he gets home by 10:30 and I can get here before 11.

A year and a half ago we started having trouble; he got a new supervisor who would not let him leave on time if his job was not done. I was told that if I was late again, I would be fired. JJ, I need this job! I have a son who is Diabetic, and he needs insulin, which is very expensive. So, a day or two later my husband called to say he had to finish fixing a leaky pipe, and he wasn't going to make his usual bus. I would have been late again. We decided that I would leave on time, because my son was asleep, and he would only be alone for 20 minutes. I felt so guilty, JJ! He is only 6! I told the neighbor so she could listen for him, but she is not well and I'm not sure she even understood what I was asking. I was so afraid when I got on the bus, I began to cry. My husband called 15 minutes later and said he was home, my son had not woken up, and everything was okay. A few days later, the same thing happened. Again, I left my son asleep and prayed that God would protect him till my husband got home. But this time, the bus was very late because of a breakdown. My son was alone for an hour! When my husband called to tell me, I was on the bus far from home and I couldn't get back any quicker than he could. I tried to call my neighbor and she did not pick up. When my husband got home, he found my boy in the hallway crying, asking for Mama or Papa." Tears streamed down Gina's face. I could have lost my son if anyone called Child Protective Services! And we would have deserved to lose him!"

"We talked about whether I should quit my job, but we needed the money. I love my job, but it does not pay very well. Finally, we decided to ask the other neighbors in the building if anyone could stay with him in an emergency. One said yes, but only if we paid on time. She charges 10 for a half an hour, 15 for an hour. So now we have to pay 20 or 30 dollars a week, which doesn't sound like much, but it is a struggle for us."

"Most of the time we can handle it, He can sometimes go in a little early for overtime and I sometimes stay late. But a couple of times the heat bill was high, and one time we dropped a vial of insulin and had to pay for a new one."

"So last year, on the day I had to buy more insulin, I came to work knowing my bank account was overdrawn, and I needed to pay thirty dollars to the babysitter when I got home. I saw Miriam's new coat, and I thought, the coat would not be needed for at least a few weeks, because it was for wintertime and then it was only October, and I thought, what if I borrow it and take it back to the store, and get cash to use for a few days, and then buy the coat back after I get paid and return it before anyone misses it? And that's what I did. I didn't think anyone had even noticed. And we did fine for a while, then a month ago the co-pay price of insulin went up from 30 to 60 dollars, and we needed the babysitter a few times that week, so I did it again with your clothes. I knew my husband would get paid extra for his overtime so I knew I could replace them. JJ, I would never have kept the money! I hope you believe that." Again, the tears flowed. "I told my husband that I can't do this again. If I get caught, I will lose my job!" But then we got our heat bill and it was very high, and they said they would turn off the heat if we did not pay it, so I returned Wayne's clothes and hoped no one would notice. But they did."

So that is why JJ, I don't know if you understand or not, but I have felt so guilty I needed to tell someone. If I get caught, I will be so embarrassed, but I will deserve it. No one would ever trust me again. Maybe it is best if it is discovered."

Gina's tears were causing wet spots on the sheets now. JJ looked at her with such sadness. He wished he could tell her he didn't care about the clothes and he was pretty sure Miriam and Wayne wouldn't either. But she was right, when it was discovered she would probably be fired.

CHAPTER 34

Thank goodness for Julie, who let him sleep late the next morning. He had laid awake staring at the ceiling for an hour after Gina's midnight confession, trying to think if there was anything to be done to help her. He knew he had money saved in his personal account. He would have given her what she needed. But generosity was one of the many things denied to him since his disability, even if he could have voiced the desire.

In all likelihood, he would be asked if he knew who had returned Wayne's clothes at some point in the near future. He wished he could say "no". If he said "yes" he knew he would be a hero to the investigator, who could finally close the case, and maybe other staff would be relieved to not be suspected. But losing Gina was like losing a part of the family! If he said no, and later Gina told people she had told him her story, everyone would think he didn't understand. That bothered him too.

In the end, he resolved, if asked, to say "NO". He would not be the reason for Gina's destruction.

He was anxious to get started on his therapy this morning. He needed to finish his SOS so someone would sit with him and hear him out. He needed several minutes to finish though, and they were trying to discourage him from using the alphabet screen, thinking he was not ready for it. Stress was starting to build in his gut. He was not used to having any responsibility, and now he was responsible two consequential secrets.

Usually Ann came around 10:30 and worked with him while he was positioning. The gooseneck arm was being designed to attach to both his headboard and his wheelchair. But as Derrick was putting him to bed at 10:15, word was sent that the device had not charged properly, having accidently been plugged into a dead outlet, and since her time would be better spent on preparing paperwork for JJ's long-term device, she would see him tomorrow.

Tomorrow might be too late, he thought. He was as miserable as he had been happy the day before. Gary seemed ready to act, and JJ could not think of another way to get help. He spent a miserable afternoon, sick with fear and dread.

JJ watched his new fish; whose name was now Triple J at Franklin's suggestion. JJ would have preferred something a little more fish-like and thought he would add changing it to the list of things to do with his new device. Triple J swam in circles in the large globe that Maria had gotten for him, and it occurred to JJ that the fish's world in some ways was larger than his. Both were confined to a specific place, but Triple J could look at a world that encompassed all 360 degrees, and JJ's was about 30 degrees.

But they shared another thing- they were both trapped. JJ indulged in a rare moment of self-pity.

JJ was in bed still when Gary walked in, about 11:45. Derrick was a little late getting him up, but JJ was glad to have a minute to monitor the creep. Gary didn't bother with a greeting for Wayne, but instead went right to the injection. His phone rang.

"Yeah? I'm here now. No, I didn't say today, I said tomorrow. Today I gave him a double dose of the Tetra, tomorrow I'll give him the insulin...because I want to give them the head's up that he's worse but not enough time to test to figure out why. I'm hoping we won't have to fight with them over an autopsy. How is mother?... Would be nice if she just died of cancer in the next few days... That one is going to be harder. We may have a problem with the kid in the next bed. He is nonverbal, and we need him to stay that way. Like I told you, if they figure it's the insulin, I have insurance to keep the focus off of me.

Gary hung up, then finished his business with Wayne and headed to the door. On his way out, he looked back at JJ. He came to the bedside leaned over and patted JJ's hand, for all the world to see looking like a kind man, but in a menacing sneer said, "You picked a lousy time to come back from the dead Lazarus. Now I have a decision to make. You better not cross me, or I'll end you when I end Wayne." With that, Gary glanced at the doorway, then scooped up Triple J with two hands and dropped him on the bedside table. JJ watched as the fish flopped around, struggling to breathe for what seemed forever, before landing somewhere on JJ's lap. Gary watched with a sneer and seemed to enjoy when a tear of both sorrow and terror dripped down JJ's cheek.

Derrick discovered Triple J a few minutes later while getting JJ up. He glanced up at JJ, who was staring at the ceiling. Derrick discretely picked the fish up without comment, and pushed the bedside table away, and JJ was sure that sometime today an identical fish would materialize in the bowl and everyone would pretend nothing happened. "Jesus", he thought, "I'm not 5".

JJ had not fully realized till just now how very dangerous his potential for communication was for Gary. He understood now that there would be no way Gary could let him tell what he knew, and if Gary was willing to kill his brother and his mother, it would be nothing to take care of JJ. What could he do to block him by tomorrow? This would be a great time for Maria to do that mind reading.

Maria discovered Wayne's clothing soon after she arrived at 4:15. She alerted Supervisor that they had reappeared, and this became the main topic of conversation at dinner time. No one had a clue what was happening. JJ would normally be smug about his inside information, but today he was miserable, pretending not to hear what was being said. He had bigger issues to worry about tonight.

At dinner, Val was busy in the kitchen and out of sight, but JJ distinctly heard a cry of protest from her. He assumed she had burnt herself or spilled something, but a second later Jason emerged with a smirk on his face, and Val followed him out, looking very angry. JJ looked at Maria and Derrick and neither had noticed. He felt his blood pressure go up. JJ had become somewhat protective of Valerie since she had broken down in front of him. She was really very good at what she did, and he felt that he and a number of others had written her off as an airhead purely because she was so pretty. He would apologize to her when he was able to use his device.

JJ was in another world all evening, not connected with what was happening in the house at all, other than an occasional glance at Valerie to see how she was doing. He was very afraid of Gary. With the introduction of the communication device he had suddenly felt very powerful, but now he felt helpless and very vulnerable. He felt like a bug about to be squashed. If Gary carried through with his plan, Wayne would be dead tomorrow, and probably him alongside.

CHAPTER 35

Gina was not on that night, just Joe and a float from another house named Lena who spent the night on her phone, according to Joe when he checked on JJ. She must be pretty bad because Joe never complained about anybody. Gina was due to come in, but Joe said she needed a mental health day.

JJ was up much of the night trying to plan a strategy, but with no real resources. He wished he had been more insistent the other day when he was using the device during therapy- he could have gotten the last few letters out and was fairly sure that at least Maria would have sat up and taken notice. He hoped the device would be there in the morning. If it was, he was going to commandeer it and get what he needed to say said before they could take it away.

The morning came and Franklin bounded into the room with his usual cheeriness. "Triple J! You, not the fish!" JJ had been right; a similar fish was now swimming in his bowl. "We are planting a garden today, so, you better be rested and ready to go!"

Normally JJ would have been all about this, but today he needed to be focused, and gardening was a distraction. Wayne was in bed- he was so weak now he had stopped eating. The MRI was scheduled for tomorrow.

As he sat watching Franklin planting tomatoes, peppers, cucumbers, and beans, asking JJJ's advice about their placement even though he had already mapped the garden out, JJ found the pleasant back yard breeze, with the smell of dirt being churned and the warmth of the sun on his arms almost offensive given his internal state of total panic. How could Franklin be calmly planting potatoes when three hours from now Wayne, and possibly he, could be dead. Franklin sensed his tension but couldn't make out the source of it. He kept up his chatter, but his glances at JJ were concerned and quizzical. If only he was the mind reader Maria was, JJ thought.

It was a wonderful sensuous morning, even if he couldn't enjoy it. As his mind raced, imagining possible endings to today's events, he caught sight of the car he'd seen the other day on the walk, parked across the street from the house. It was hard to tell through the trees, but it looked empty. Then he saw him, the driver, on the edge of his visual field, seeming to conceal himself behind a car. It looked to be him- same stature anyway. He again looked very familiar. JJ felt a chill; was the man watching him, or Franklin, or the new guy? The new guy had not been on the walk the other day, and neither had Franklin. If he was watching JJ, who was he? A friend of Brad's (it wasn't Brad) or was its Gary's brother? Both would not wish him well. He couldn't see the face from where he was, and as he tried to focus, the man turned his back and got back in his car and drove away. On a scale of 1 to 10, JJ's fear had been a 10, now it was a 20.

At 10:15 after a quick snack Franklin put JJ back into bed. "I hope you're not getting sick J; you don't seem yourself." Franklin felt his forehead and looked at him for a moment. JJ waited for Ann desperately, or rather the device she would be bringing, and almost gave up on her in despair when she breezed in with someone she introduced as the "Adaptive Equipment Specialist", Rodney. They were excited about the new gooseneck stand Rodney had fabricated for JJ, which allowed the device to be positioned in front of him whether in the bed or in the wheelchair. His forty-five-minute therapy session was mostly used up by Rodney and Ann discussing its function, tweaking it, then bringing in Supervisor and Franklin for training. As they explained its mounting hardware and positioning, JJ quickly opened up the alphabet screen and added ...g... to the word.

Ann laughed. "JJ can't wait to get me out of the way so he can use this thing! You're "urging" me to go home, right?" No that was not right. He was going to be so glad to not have people guessing what he meant.

'Just let me at it', he thought. " It is a matter of life and death."

"Just give us another minute to show Franklin how it goes on your chair, then I'll get out of your way."

He would have a half hour before lunch, and he thought he could get the word out by then. The device was left with him at last, and Franklin repositioned JJ back in his chair for lunch. He was down to fifteen minutes. He managed to type the e and n before Franklin pushed his chair to the lunch table, and JJ found it impossible to operate it in motion. When he finally stopped at the table, JJ tried to save the word, but Franklin accidently bumped his chair and JJ activated erase by mistake, instead of save, losing the two new letters.

JJ was panicked now, his heart racing as he realized how little time he had. He put back the "e" and the "n" and started on the "t", when lunch arrived. He tried to ignore lunch and continue, but Franklin didn't understand and very firmly said, "JJ, you need to eat- I promise we'll go back to it right afterwards. OK?" JJ wanted to scream NO! but he realized better to eat quickly and get it over with, then to risk having the device taken away. He swallowed as quickly as he could and ate only until Franklin seemed satisfied, then went back to his mission.

He found the "t" and hit speak, with a huge wave of relief. But nothing happened. He tried again. Nothing. He went to the home page and selected "I don't know" just to test it. It did not make a sound. No one was paying attention to him or his board.

Franklin was talking to Supervisor and cleaning up. He patted JJ's hand and said "Taking a break J. Will put you down when I get back. You can practice with your machine till I get back." And he left without a second look.

JJ was near tears. It had been a long time since he had used electronic devices and he was trying to troubleshoot based on 10-year-old memory. He finally realized the problem might be the volume and began to look for the volume control. Was there a mechanical control, or was there a setting he needed to fix? He searched but the device demanded precision that was still difficult for him. Scanning the options and then settling his gaze on the correct one yielded wrong choice time and again. Supervisor came in the front door and JJ startled when the door shut, rattling his tray and causing others to look up. "You ok, J?" Derrick asked, but he was busy feeding Michael, so he didn't come over.

Finally, Franklin came back. "Let's give your butt a rest JJ!" Franklin joked as he disengaged the brakes of his wheelchair and pushed him back to his room. JJ tried to pull up the alphabet screen; maybe if Franklin saw the word he would understand and help. But he could not do anything with the chair in motion, he couldn't hold his gaze steady enough. Franklin carried on a monologue as he got JJ in bed. It occurred to JJ it might be harder to get people to stop talking at him and start listening to him than he thought. As Franklin settled him into bed and reset the device so it was in JJ's sight, he saw that JJ was in the settings. "JJ you don't want to be in there. I don't have a clue how to fix it if you screw it up." Franklin clicked out of the settings page and returned to the home page. Without waiting for a response, Franklin said, "see you tomorrow J" and left the room. JJ wondered if tomorrow he would be telling the story and saying "...and that was the last time I saw him alive..."

It was after 2- Gary was usually here and gone by now. Maybe he wasn't coming today, maybe he changed his mind and couldn't go through with it. JJ tried to stay calm and kept at his device, going back into the settings page. He found the volume control, but it required precision to operate that was impossible for him this early in his training.

The clock ticked on. He could hear Wayne snoring. Did he have a clue what could happen this afternoon? Was he aware of what Gary had in mind? If he did, he showed no concern. Had he resigned himself to it? Did he welcome it? Thanks to Gary, Wayne could hardly pick up his head.

Finally, JJ gave up on the settings and went back to the alphabet screen. He began to type. He would make his statement, so that even if he didn't live someone would discover his message and hold Gary accountable. He began to find the letters.....G.......a........r.... progress was painstakingly slow.....

It was after 3 and Gary still had not arrived. JJ started to relax a little-maybe Gary was all talk and had no intention of hurting Wayne or him. He started revisiting the conversation he had overheard word by word:

"I said tomorrow. Today I gave him a double dose of the Tetra, tomorrow I'll give him the insulin...because I want to give them the head's up that he's worse but not enough time to test to figure out why. I'm hoping we won't have to fight with them over an autopsy. How is mother?... Would be nice if she just died of cancer in the next few days... That one is going to be harder. We may have a problem with the kid in the next bed. He is nonverbal, and we need him to stay that way. Like I told you, if they figure out it's the insulin, I have insurance to keep the focus off of me."

Not much room for misunderstanding there. What did he mean "insurance"?

....y....g.....a.....v....e.....

JJ suddenly stopped. It all made sense to him now...Gary stealing the syringe that day when Maria was doing meds...and Gary being late today.... He was waiting for Maria to start her shift... He was going to pin it on her!

JJ continued, this time with renewed effort- W....a....y....n...e.... and as the clock finally arrived at 4:00, Gary walked into the room.

He looked at JJ, then walked over to Wayne. He did not look as sure-fire cocky as he usually did but seemed nervous and spoke to Wayne quietly. JJ could not hear everything, but what he heard sounded a bit like an apology for what he was about to do, and an assurance that his Mom would be with him soon. He was moving around, and JJ could picture the insulin being pushed into his blood stream. JJ did not know exactly what to expect from insulin poisoning, but he closed his eyes and tried to still his heartbeat as he tried not to cry. He remembered this may be the last chance to leave his message and quickly returned to his task. I....n....s....u...l... but suddenly Gary was right there. His resolve seemed stronger- JJ was a stranger, easier to kill. He whispered, "sorry kid, you were in the wrong room at the wrong time...." And he pulled out a gloved hand with a syringe. He drew up a full syringe of insulin and quickly pushed the needle into JJ's abdomen. He then dropped the syringe on the bed, "your friend Maria will be discovered as an angel killer trying to put two of her favorite people out of their misery. Everyone will say they never saw it coming. Don't worry, you'll be gone soon, and no one will miss you. You've got to admit, your life is pretty lame anyway." Gary smiled broadly as he said this and patted JJ's hand. Pure evil with a friendly face.

He began to step away then saw the message JJ had spent the last hour composing. He looked at it, then JJ, and said "impressive! Guess they were right about you!" He found the backspace and erased hours of JJ's work. He swung the gooseneck away from the bed, then released the clamp, and holding the device over his head smashed it the ground. He looked over at the mess and said "that's a shame! You were just getting the hang of it!" Footsteps pounded in the hall- and Gary pretended to have run over to the debris, his gloved hands stuffed in his pockets, just as the door flew open and Maria burst in.

"Oh, sweet Jesus! JJ! How did this happen?" Maria was devastated by the wreckage of the $8,000 device. Gary shrugged and said, "I'm not sure. I was with Wayne when I heard the crash. Must be it wasn't installed properly?" Gary guessed. Mona and Valerie were right behind Maria, and the three of them inspected the disaster as Gary slipped out.

JJ felt himself slipping away as well. He heard Maria as she busied herself picking up, but she had little to say. She seemed to be annoyed at Franklin for his carelessness and was trying not to take it out on JJ. She cleaned up, gave him the treatment to his hands, and stepped out with the med cart. She did not notice as he slipped into semi-consciousness.

Fifteen minutes later she returned after finishing medications and found both Wayne and JJ unresponsive.

CHAPTER 36

The ambulance sirens blared, and JJ was dimly aware of them as he lapsed in and out of consciousness. The face of Maria also blinked in and out, and her tears rolled on to his face as she held it with her hands and begged him to stay with her. Then he slipped away.

When his eyes fluttered open again, he had no idea how much time had passed. Was he dead? He stared up at the ceiling above him. He had been in this position before, after the accident- dull, confused, dreamlike. In and out, for what seemed like days but may have been hours or even minutes. Gradually, memory of what had happened returned. He wondered about Wayne. He struggled to think- his chest hurt with every breath, his eyes burned with the light of the room and he kept them shut for a while. Soothing voices in the room telling him to relax, they were going to put him back to sleep for a while so they could remove the ventilator, then again darkness.

The periods of wakefulness gradually came more often and lasted a little longer each time; in between wakefulness, long periods of sleep. He dreamt of his mother, and Maria, and of opening his eyes and seeing his Dad.

After a day or two, his brain fog cleared, and he was able to follow what was happening. Supervisor came, then Molly, each patting his arm, telling him he was going to get better, and talking to the nurses and Doctors as they checked on him. He pieced together information little by little...insulin poisoning... sugar dropped to 23...organ failure...may need dialysis if kidneys didn't begin to function...not sure yet of any brain damage....

And Wayne: the same, but worse.

CHAPTER 37

He felt stronger and clearer the next time he woke up. Franklin's face appeared over him with a big smile.

"Triple J! Welcome back! Mona said you had woken up this morning! I been here every day, I swear! Been worried about you, bro!" Franklin squeezed his hand and raised his bed a little.

Franklin kept up his usual one-sided conversation, pausing to ask for "yes" responses, which JJ was still too foggy to give. Franklin apologized tearfully about not mounting the device correctly and ruining everything for J, "Hell, J, you might even have been able to call for help!"

Franklin said they had not decided what they were going to do about him, because Administration was upset he had caused the loss of the equipment, "but they knew it was my first time, and they know I was trying to be careful, so I don't think it will be too bad. Maybe a letter in my file. I just feel bad for you J. I let you down."

"But right now, we have to focus on you. Getting you better so we can get you out of here. I had lunch in the cafeteria yesterday. A hamburger! God, J, don't let them feed you that stuff! I'll smuggle you in a Big Mac or something!" JJ would not be getting food anytime soon, but he smirked. It was good to hear Franklin being Franklin.

Then Franklin pulled his chair up close to J and leaned over so J could see his face. "Ok, man, I probably shouldn't lay this on you yet, but I gotta know, do you know who did this to you and Wayne? JJ deliberately rolled his eyes to the right.

"Was it Maria?" Franklin asked softly. JJ stared at him, glaring. "I knew it! I knew it!" Franklin smiled, relieved. "They kept saying there was no other explanation, and I said there had to be! That woman wouldn't hurt anyone, much less someone she loves like she loves you, J!" He went on to say that Maria had screamed for help when she found the two of them. In the haste to get them to the hospital, bedding was left on the floor, and when Joe had picked it up for the wash, he had found the syringe. Lab tests revealed it had been used for both JJ and Wayne, and Maria's prints were the only ones (other than Joe's) on it. So, they arrested her. She's in jail because she couldn't make bail. JJ's eyes nearly exploded with rage-Maria, in jail! While Gary walked free?

"I don't want to upset you, JJ, probably shouldn't have told you this. Don't worry, there has to be some way to prove she didn't do it. Everyone who knows her knows she couldn't. We're trying to raise bail money to get her out. But all they say is it happened before- staff who are so caring think they're helping by putting people out of their misery. But Maria knew you weren't miserable. You were just getting started. That communication device is going to be primo for you J. You can finally tell Jason off!" Already on it, thought JJ. I'll have to set up a new F-U file.

Ann is getting you a new communication device and maybe you'll be able to help clear Maria. Again, I'm sorry about yours. I was so sure I had it on right. Remember I even tugged on it to make sure it was tight? Damn, don't know what I did wrong!"

"Well they told me I couldn't stay long because you need to rest. Oh, by the way, I got to admit maybe Gary's not the creep I thought he was. He's been here every day to look in on Wayne and you. Seems very concerned. He keeps asking to visit you, but they said only a few of us can. Julia is doing bedside staffing with Wayne, so he just pops his head in- Wayne isn't doing as well as you, J."

With his hand on the door, he started to leave when he paused, "and J, I don't know if you want to see him or not, but your father has been here every day."

CHAPTER 38

JJ lay thinking about what he'd learned. How anyone could think sweet Maria capable of murder was unfathomable. He knew that Gary was planning to pin it on her, but never thought the charge would get traction. His heart broke to think of her in jail!

And why has no one thought of Gary? JJ figured the best way to get away with murder was to wear a nice suit. Were he and Franklin the only ones who realized what a creep the guy was? And now he's playing the concerned brother. Concerned that he didn't get it right the first time, maybe, JJ thought. But if he got another chance, he wouldn't screw it up. JJ was suddenly very afraid. He realized his present room was monitored by camera. Gary would have to wait till he moved to another unit.

Supervisor came in and sat with him that afternoon for a long time. She was looking older and more tired, and JJ felt sorry for her. She told him about Maria, as gently as she could because she knew how close they'd been. She said she herself didn't believe it, but the only other one around at the time was Gary, and the prints on the syringe were Maria's, not Gary's. She hoped there would be another explanation. Anne was working double time to try to get a new device for him because the authorities felt JJ was the most important piece of evidence they had. The prosecution thought it would clinch the case, the house staff hoped he could clear Maria.

Supervisor had been at the house when JJ arrived seven years ago. She had a reputation for taking great pride in her house, insisting her staff be professional and attentive to the people they supported, and having a deep reservoir of experience to draw from. Her staff were a little fearful of her but very loyal, and proud of themselves for being good enough for Mona.

JJ agreed with all those who felt that way about her. He had always kept her at arm's length, being unwilling to trust her too much. He had moved here from a nursing home facility where care was spotty at best. Staff came and went, and he learned to not make relationships with people who had no intention of sticking around. When he first arrived, Mona had taken great pains to make him comfortable and supported him in many ways, but his distrust kept him from letting her get too close emotionally. He had called her Supervisor because in his experience in the system, titles were a constant, people not so much.

As he got to know staff like Franklin, Maria, even Derrick and Julie, his reserve melted, and he became just one of the Cedar Hills gang. But he'd always kept his distance from Mona mentally and just thought of her as Supervisor. As she sat there, worried about the same people he worried about, he figured that by now she had earned his trust and he owed it to her to give her a name.

He napped on and off throughout the afternoon. At one point his eyes fluttered open and he saw his Dad standing over him holding his hand. He closed his eyes quickly before his Dad could start to talk to him. He wasn't ready for that kind of conversation.

CHAPTER 39

Another day and he was feeling better. He heard from Franklin that Wayne was out of danger too, so Gary would be anxious to finish the job, JJ thought. JJ was due to be moved the next day, as soon a bed opened up on a regular unit. He knew that he would be assigned bed side staff, so he would be protected most of every day. He wished Ann would hurry up with that device, because he might finally run out of luck as Gary got more desperate.

That night his Dad stopped in again. He was a bit stronger, and kept his eyes open, but straight ahead.

"I know you probably don't want to see me James, and I really don't blame you. I've been stopping by the house to check on you from a distance, but I didn't think I'd be welcome so stayed away. It made me feel better to see that you seemed happy." He paused, half expecting a response, but JJ just stared at the wall. So, the mysterious man was his dad.

"I apologize for not being there for you for so long, but I realize that my feeling bad doesn't mean you'll feel any better. I really fell apart after the last time I saw you. When was that now? Five or six years?" his Dad cleared his throat and he seemed to need to compose himself before continuing.

"So, I drank myself into the hospital. When they let me out, I had lost my job and I lived on the street for years, pretty much drunk. But a year ago I ended up in a hospital again. A therapist was trying to get me to talk about my reasons for drinking and I told her about you, and how when Mom died, I let you fend for yourself instead of taking care of you. It was my fault you had the accident and were left with basically no life. So, she asked me to tell her about you. I told her where you live, and that the staff who worked with you said you had a good sense of humor, and seemed to be happy there, and how much they loved you. And the Therapist said to me "Sounds like your son is doing ok. You're the one without a life."

"And she was right. While I'm feeling sorry for myself and no good to anyone you moved on and made the life you have the best it can be. You were so much stronger than I was. And I was very ashamed of myself."

JJ turned his eyes towards his father. He wasn't sure yet what to think of his words- sounded like he was still self-pitying. But he was surprised to see his father dry eyed, with his head held high, and calm.

"So, I gave myself a swift kick in the butt. I started going to meetings at AA and stopped drinking. One of the things they teach is to make amends to those you hurt. And I will, in any way you want me to, until I die, I promise JJ. Another thing they teach is that other people don't have to forgive you, and I understand you may not."

So, this was a Twelve Step assignment, JJ thought. He had heard of this before. A former staff had gone to the program to get clean and he came and gave this same speech. JJ was not impressed.

"But I also have come to love and respect myself again JJ. I have a job as a maintenance man at the apartment complex where I live. I have a car; I have a few friends. So, whatever you decide to do regarding our relationship, I know you'll be ok, and I want you to know I'll be ok. I think your mother would be very proud of both of us today J. I'll come see you, and you can tell me whether or not you want me to stay. But I promise I'll keep coming. See you tomorrow James." And he patted JJ's hand as he left.

JJ lay in his bed for a while just thinking, staring at the ceiling. He was still very angry at his Dad, but he couldn't help but feel it would be nice if he was telling the truth. He did look and sound different today. JJ was afraid to hold out much hope-time would tell. Unfortunately, time would also tell whether JJ would be around for this family reunion. Every minute brought JJ to a showdown with Gary, and Gary had all the cards. He could not let JJ live, and he knew it.

CHAPTER 40

Gina came to see him that evening. She was suspended from work, but her husband was home, so she had the time.

In the end, she said she could not live with herself. She spoke to Mona and Debra and told them everything. They were very understanding but she still thought, in all likelihood, she'd be fired. Mona told her she had pleaded for Human Resources to show leniency, but they were pretty adamant that company policy was no tolerance for theft.

Gina fussed with him a bit, cutting his nails and washing his face. She told him he would always be one of her favorite people. And if she did lose her job, she wanted him to know how much she cared for and admired him.

By the time she left JJ was an emotional bowl of jello. He typically avoided dwelling on deep emotions and now he was neck deep in them. And still no Ann. He needed that device. Tomorrow would be another day of waiting for the inevitable end to this story. He almost wished he would spike a fever so he could stay in the ICU.

But no such luck. Bright and early the next day an orderly showed up with a nurse to get him packed up, and he was whisked down to Unit 6c. a general care unit. And to make it easier on the agency staff, he was put in the same room as Wayne.

JJ was trembling as they transferred him to the new bed, and the nurse mistakenly thought he was cold and said she would get some warm blankets. As she left the room his privacy curtain was pushed aside, and Gary stepped in.

"Sorry about all this kid. Didn't intend you to suffer a long, prolonged death. Not to worry! Next time will be very quick!"

The nurse walked in and in a voice rich with irony Gary said "what a relief to see this guy looking so much better! I've been seeing him daily for months now, I feel like he's family!" The nurse smiled at him. She didn't know how he treated his family.

When they were left alone Gary sauntered over to the bed and spoke in a low voice, "what to do, what to do.....I know you are just bursting to tell everyone what you know, and I know that that therapist of yours is trying to find another communication device for you, so you will understand if we have to move quickly. I screwed up- I should have used more insulin. Wayne will have to hang around a bit longer. I wouldn't dare try again so soon. But you have to go soon. I know what you're capable of unfortunately. But don't worry, I intend to be at the nurse's station when it happens. You will finally get to meet my brother you've heard so much about." He wandered back to Wayne's bed. "Oh, and Maria was bailed out today. I contributed a substantial amount to the staff bail fund. Hopefully she won't have an alibi this time. I sent a message for her to meet Mona here this afternoon."

Joe was in today and he was his usual sweet, slow self. He was good company, and they watched a couple of shows together. Or rather Joe watched them. JJ stared straight ahead and tried to pray for divine intervention. He should probably do this more often, he thought. He was very rusty. About every hour Joe needed to use the guest bathroom, which was down the hall, and each trip took 10 to 15 minutes.

Gary had gone to work shortly after his threat to JJ, but around 3:00 he reappeared. He nodded to Joe, then killed time at Wayne's bedside, on his phone with an occasional remark directed towards Wayne for Joe's sake.

Around 3:45 Joe stretched and announced another trip to the bathroom. As soon as the door closed Gary stood, punched something into his phone, and headed to the nursing station, saying "Good-Bye JJ" on his way out. JJ tried to claw his fingers in the direction of the call button. He had never been able to use it before, but he would try. He fumbled with the wire, trying to pull the button through his fingers, but he was way too slow.

A second later his door opened, and a man JJ had never seen before slinked to his bed. This man was nothing like Gary. He was short, dressed in a wrinkled shirt and a pair of jeans, balding on the top of his head, and spectacles on his nose. He looked as frightened as JJ felt, fumbling in his pocket with gloved hands for a syringe, avoiding eye contact, trying to hurry but not succeeding. He finally got the cap off, looked at JJ and mumbled "I'm sorry" and held the syringe to JJ's abdomen to inject.

In their joint fear neither of them had seen the door open and JJ's Dad step in. He quickly assessed the situation, grabbed the man by both shoulders, and threw him to the ground. The man made a weak stab at J's Dad with the syringe, but he easily flicked it away and put him in a head lock while pressing the call button with his other hand. JJ was not sure the call would be answered before Joe or Gary got back, the nurses didn't always jump, but his Dad wasn't waiting, he was backing towards the door, dragging the man with him. He made it to the door just as it was opened by Joe, who took a minute to process the scene and yell for security.

The needle had pricked JJ's skin, but no injection had occurred. Joe and the Nurse looked him over carefully. JJ felt his whole body take a deep breath in relief. It was over.

Security arrived, relieved JJ's Dad of his prisoner, and collected the syringe.

JJ stared at his Dad with the wonder of his 8-year-old self. His Dad was his hero.

CHAPTER 41

The man's name was William, Wayne's oldest brother. He was a weak, whiny little thing who was confessing to his role and Gary's almost before Security took him into custody. JJ could hear him in the hall, spilling his guts. The story came back to JJ from various staff in bits and pieces, filling in the parts he didn't already know.

He and his brother were made aware of their Mother's cancer six months ago. Gary had looked at the will and discovered the estate to be worth about 3.3 million. He was upset to realize that she had given a third of it to Wayne. Gary said Wayne needed to die before his mother because if it happened afterwards the state would take his inheritance. When Gary screwed up the first attempt, he came up with the idea of his brother finishing up JJ. William was suspicious that his brother might set him up to take the fall as he had Maria. William claimed he had recorded some of their conversations in case he needed insurance against that happening.

William claimed he was not greedy and would have been fine with a three-way split but was afraid if he didn't cooperate Gary may decide to get rid of him too. He withheld some of the insulin from his mother daily and replaced it with water. Their plan was to use insulin poisoning because Gary believed it was not identifiable upon autopsy. He had weakened Wayne with tetra hydroxide for a couple of months. He didn't want to kill him until he had established himself as an involved, loving brother, and he wanted the house to see him decline so his death would not be totally unexpected. The plan was an overdose of insulin when enough time had elapsed. His only worry had been being caught, and when he happened upon the medication procedure of disposing of the syringe in the trash on top of the med cart, he had the confidence to go through with it. But the dose he gave was not enough, and they both pulled through. He was afraid to try again because it might cast suspicion on himself, so he contributed to the staff fund to get Maria bailed out and left her a message from the hospital phone that Mona needed to see her at the hospital. She was in the lobby when everything had happened. Cameras would have shown her there, and the frame up would have been complete. Except that JJ's dad arrived in time to screw it all up.

According to the security guard Gary had heard the scuffle and left by the back stairs. The police got the story from William and grabbed Gary as he pulled into his own driveway.

JJ came home the next day, and Wayne a day later. There were balloons and a welcome home cake, and this time everyone got to have a piece. The house seemed lighter to JJ, even though he was the only one who had born the secret, the whole house seemed unburdened

Ann came with the new device the next morning after driving to a sister agency up north to get it. When William told the police that JJ had typed his SOS and Gary had destroyed the machine to prevent JJ from communicating again, it gave her chills to realize how important it had been. And all this time she thought they would be working on expressing simple choices and storing commonly used phrases, not sending out pleas for help. She told JJ that he was now in charge of his therapy, she would be there as a consultant to teach him how to use the machine.

JJ had pretty much forgiven everything his Dad had ever done. The man he saw in the hospital room was the man JJ knew as a child. He started visiting every day or two, and often sat and had dinner with J and his peers and staff. His first name was Jerome Johnson and Franklin nicknamed him Double J, which his Dad thought was very funny. JJ thought there was a little spark between Mona and his Dad, but he didn't want to intrude by asking- time would tell.

Maria came back to work. She was mortified about having been in jail, but everyone surrounded her with support and she tearfully thanked all of them for their trust and helping with bail, each time eliciting tears and hugs all over again.

JJ's Dad told him one day "These people are our family now, James. Love is what makes a family. Your mom would have loved all of them. He leaned close and said, "except Jason," and winked.

CHAPTER 42

It was weeks later, and JJ's device included dozens of icons on its main page, and more saved phrases each of which JJ laboriously typed and stored for future use. "I'm hungry" "I'm not hungry" "Maria, would you feed Murky" (the fish's new name) and "Franklin, do I have to tell Mona about the mattress?" The latter was an inside joke, and though Mona begged he would not reveal its meaning.

On the next rainy day, he told staff to check behind the bookcase, and when they did so and retrieved the lost nature DVDs a cheer went up from the grateful-they would never hear the words "robin red breast" again.

Mona was offered the Assistant Director position and accepted it, so the interviews for her job were being scheduled. Maria put in for it, as did Franklin, though he said he was just doing it for practice, because he knew Maria was a shoo in. Jason also put in for it, probably just to irritate Mona. Some others from other houses also submitted but JJ was hoping they would hire from within.

Gina came back from her suspension. Mona was able to get her punishment down to an extended probation and a disciplinary letter. In completing the investigation, it was discovered that due to a misspelling of her name, a number of cost-of-living raises were missed, so not only was she going to make 1.75 more an hour, she was owed back pay to the tune of 1,500.

Jason continued to be the bastard he'd always been. One day before Mona left, he cornered Valerie in a hallway and sexually harassed her. On his way out the door on yet another suspension that night, JJ was able to use his "Jason, fuck off" icon. He had raised the volume so that it was heard throughout the dining room and got a raucous laugh until Mona came out to usher Jason out the door and admonish everyone. "JJ you've had your fun, now delete that." Which he did. Mona assured everyone that Jason would not be coming back.

The only thing left causing stress was Maria's court case against Brad. His lawyer was claiming that there was no evidence, other than Maria's statement, that an assault had happened. He accused her of cutting herself and leaving the marks on her own neck just to set him up. Mona did not actually see him, there were no other witnesses, and with no other evidence, Brad might walk.

Ann came with Debbie Mullen who was working with the lawyer to frame the questions likely to be asked. JJ was told to use the yes/no functions on his device, because it was felt by the Prosecutor that JJ's slow key activation could be misread as lack of confidence in his answers. So, they rehearsed. "Were you present when a man entered your room with a knife held to Maria's neck and a hand over her mouth?" Yes. Was this the man? (hold up a picture of Brad) Yes. "Did Brad push Maria back on the bed." Yes. They hoped if the answers were quick it would sound credible. It was difficult to guess how a jury would react to such a disabled person with an electronic voice.

But JJ had his own opinion of how best to speak for Maria. He worked nightly on his own statement during the weeks leading up to the trial. He had watched a lot of Law and Order over the last few years, not for nothing. Maria was very nervous leading up to the court case. JJ was too, but he felt prepared. Brad couldn't walk.

CHAPTER 43

The morning of the trial came after numerous cancelations and hearings, and JJ had successfully pleaded with his nurse and Mona to attend the whole thing. The deal he made was that he would be out of his wheelchair and in alternative positioning at all times when home, and he could attend all day as long as his skin showed no signs of breakdown. So, he sat through a full day of opening statements, with Franklin nervously fidgeting by his side. The prosecutor presented Maria as a saint, who had lousy taste in men and had supported Brad for months after he lost his job, in spite of regular physical assaults, usually when he was drunk. He would present numerous character witnesses and neighbors who would testify to hearing his assaults.

The Defense attorneys painted Maria as an overly dramatic clingy woman who was always drumming up sympathy by playing the victim. She was upset with Brad because he had approached her at work and tried to talk to her. When she realized he wouldn't be arrested for that she fabricated an attack. He promised to present a character witness in the form of Brad's present girlfriend who would testify he was never abusive (they had been together for four weeks).

While anyone who knew Maria would have no doubt about the true scenario, the jurors did not know Maria and JJ could see how persuasive the Defense Attorney could be.

If Brad got away with this, he didn't think Maria would ever feel safe, and JJ's sense of justice would never be satisfied.

CHAPTER 44

Day 1's witness lineup was a series of neighbors who heard screaming, what sounded like blows, slamming doors etc. Maria was such a sweetheart, Brad seemed to have a bad temper. A few character witnesses from work, two of which had been there the night of the assault. The neighbor who had held Brad off the week before the assault. A very consistent picture of a violent, ill-tempered man.

But cross examination turned a lot of impressions around. Maria was said to be miserable with Brad, but never left him. She could have been the one delivering the blows and slamming the doors. They couldn't say for sure. The work witnesses had to admit their only knowledge of the incident came from Maria herself. The neighbor couldn't be sure that Brad intended to harm her, instead of just trying to talk. By the time he was done, JJ wasn't sure what the jury thought.

And the next day Maria testified. She talked about how they met and how sweet he was to her. She believed it was his abuse of alcohol that made him violent, and she begged him to get treatment. She hated to leave him because she felt if he could stop drinking, she would get back the man she loved, but he refused. She finally left him when his pushing and shoving turned to punching and slapping. He did not take it well and pursued her at work and eventually attacked her at work in front of JJ. She described how the urine spill had distracted him and allowed her to scream for help, and he had run out the back door before Mona had come in response to her screams.

JJ thought she did well, but she was a bit timid upon cross examination and not as forceful as JJ thought she should have sounded. He was not at all confident.

Next up was JJ. The jury was respectful and obviously curious. The questioning went as they had rehearsed. He was asked yes/no questions and he responded. He did exactly as asked, with reasonably quick response time. The prosecutor was very satisfied.

The Defense Attorney had to be careful, he couldn't make JJ seem credible, but he also couldn't be too rough, or it would turn off the jury. He was informed that JJ would only answer yes/no questions, so made a show of asking open ended questions, only to apologize and struggle to rephrase it as a yes/no. The message was clear: he could not properly cross-examine this witness. He made the point of JJ's narrow vision very clearly. Again, the message was: this person is very limited, and his opinion or observations should be viewed as such. JJ felt that he was not doing badly, but he wasn't sure what the jury thought. Then the Defense Attorney said he was done, sighing as if he wished he could have asked more. The judge began to give instruction when JJ switched to his stored phrases and selected one that said " Your honor, may I make a statement I've prepared? I type slowly so I have spent a great deal of time preparing it."

The whole court room, including the Prosecutor and Defense Attorney's table, was taken aback. The judge thought for a moment, then asked the Prosecutor, who consulted with Maria. Maria was shaking her head "yes", but the prosecutor was not so sure. Finally, Maria won: "we have no objection." The Defense Attorney was even more hesitant and began to sputter about having not had opportunity to review this information, but the judge chided him and said, I will allow, and if there is information that is irrelevant to these proceedings, I will instruct the jury to ignore.

JJ selected the stored file and sat back and watched the reaction of Maria and Brad. Over Maria's head, in the back of the room he saw his father, and it made him feel surprisingly more confident.

The room was deathly quiet as the electronic voice gave a calm, clear, concise description of the events of that day from beginning to end.

" On April 23rd Maria came to work at 4:00. When she was getting me ready for the evening, I saw a bruise on her cheek. She told me she had called out sick the day before because her boyfriend had gotten upset and hit her, so she had left him. The same day we were taking a walk and her boyfriend drove by us, slammed on his brakes and came after us. I can only see straight in front of me, but I hear well. I saw him when he got out of the car, and I heard him running towards us as we ran to our house and I heard our neighbor tell him to leave us alone. The next day

Maria was on duty we were in my room when we heard a knock on the side door. Maria was changing my urine bag at the time and she left it on the bed while she answered the door. I can see the door to my room, so I saw Brad push Maria into my room with his right hand on Maria's throat and a knife in his left hand pressed against her neck. He was wearing a blue polo shirt and sunglasses. I heard him push her on the bed and tell her he was going to kill her. I can pull myself up with my left hand a little bit and I did that, enough to see Brad standing over her on the bed and tell her he was trying to decide whether to kill her by cutting her throat or by strangling her. As I pulled myself up, I knocked over the bag of urine that Maria had left on the bed and it fell to the floor, spilling urine over the floor and I believe Brad's feet. I believe that because I heard Brad yell "Fuck" and he stopped strangling Maria. She got away from him and screamed for help. I know that because she made it to the door where I could see her. I saw him drag her back to the bed by her hair, then look upset because the floor was wet. He pushed her down and left the room. I heard him go out the side door. A few seconds later Mona and Valerie came into the room and helped Maria.

I promise that I have prepared this statement by myself without any assistance from anyone, and that it is 100% true and accurate. Thank you, your honor."

Maria and the Prosecutor beamed. The Defense table conferenced for a minute and then sullenly said "Your honor may we be seen in chambers?"

The judge agreed. An hour later Brad had changed his plea to guilty in exchange for a reduced sentence of five years.

CHAPTER 45

JJ was roundly credited with what they all saw as a victory, though the Prosecutor told him to never surprise a Prosecutor like that again. Maria, Mona, Franklin and JJ went out to dinner to celebrate, and his Dad joined them as a surprise.

After replaying the trial over and over again, Mona changed the subject and made the announcement that she had chosen her replacement. All eyes turned towards Maria.

"I have had excellent options, but I have chosen Franklin."

Franklin was stunned-this was the first time he'd heard it, and he looked immediately at Maria.

"Congratulations!" she beamed at him and gave him a hug.

"Maria made this a very easy decision Franklin. She withdrew her name."

"I'm going back to school. Only part time, but I don't want to take on a new job while I'm taking classes. I'm going to be a nurse!" Maria explained.

Franklin looked stunned. "Are you sure, Mona? Do you think I'm ready?

"I know you're not ready, but I know what I'm getting Franklin. I don't think there is another person who makes our house more fun and who cares more about the people who live there, and no one who works harder. You have compassion and a real knack for bringing the best out in people. I can't teach those skills to other people. I can teach you what you need to know about procedures and paperwork and policies. But you will have to start following the straight and narrow. And I'll coach you. And by the way, I want you to tell Miriam yourself. She is going to be thrilled. She told me to "Hire Franklin, Mona, he won't screw it up". Everyone raised their glasses to Franklin, and JJ found out he really liked Riesling.

CHAPTER 46

The next day almost seemed a bit dull. Nothing big was happening. They were outside to pick some of the first vegetables from the garden. Wayne and JJ were "helping", Wayne holding the basket on his wheelchair tray, and JJ was trash talking Franklin's gardening skills with his communication device.

From behind, JJ heard his Dad's voice, and was startled by a large tongue licking his face. "Scout!" He couldn't believe it. His dad had said he had given Scout to a neighbor ten years ago, but here he was. Scout seemed to remember him; he couldn't stop wagging his tail and nuzzling JJ's arm.

"Mr. Jenson is in his 80's and feels it would be better if Scout came back to my house. Franklin says he can come here any time he wants." JJ spent the afternoon being nuzzled and licked, and in between times programming commands and phrases for Scout. "Good boy Scout." Come, Scout," "Not in the house, Scout!" Wayne seemed to love the hairy beast as well, and Miriam pulled her wheelchair around to follow him throughout the house. By the time his Dad left Franklin was calling Mona to see who he would have to speak to for permission to have a dog in the house.

After his Dad left and he was put down for afternoon positioning, JJ lay in bed with a deep sense of contentment. He was going to ask to have a computer that was gaze operated purchased. One advantage of having a sedentary lifestyle was even at 35 dollars spending money a month, he had saved up enough money. Maybe he would even think about taking a class on-line. Franklin was getting him a Google Home, and he said he could just tell it what to do, and it would turn on his lights, tv, make phone calls, etc.

When Valerie came in to get him up, he asked what was for dinner. "Meatloaf", Val answered.

"Who cooked? JJ asked.

"Derrick. "

JJ clicked on his saved phrases page: "Please order me a pizza."

Valerie stood back and looked at him and shook her head. "You, sir, are going to be trouble. What do you want on it?"

That night when he was back in bed, he started on another preset phrase. When he finished, he tested it out.

"Would someone take care of this damn fly?"

He would be ready for the next time.

A NOTE FROM THE AUTHOR

I first met a person with a disability when I was 14, as a volunteer teaching swimming to children. I fell in love with the kids I taught- children with a zest for life, with hearts open to love and eager to experience all that life offered. In short, they were just like all the other kids I met.

That was the beginning of my career, a 50-year-long meandering through the field of human services, providing direct support, counseling, teaching, supervising residential and day programs, and ultimately whole programs of services dedicated to ensuring all people get to experience life to the fullest. That first impression I had when I was a teenager was born out throughout all those years: in their diversity of abilities, of aspirations, of races, ages, and economic status, they are the same as all of us. We share a need for love and acceptance, and while some may need more support throughout their lives, all of us need support at times.

The other thing I learned about the field of disabilities is that it attracts some of the kindest, most giving, creative people in the world. I have often been star struck at the ability of a direct support staff or clinician to connect with an individual in need of support and use their special skills to transform someone's life and be transformed by the experience.

The circumstances of those in group residences vary-some individuals come from active, involved families who just need a little support to make it all work. For some, there is no family and staff and peers must fill that void. For some individuals, the line between paid caregivers and family blur, and we encompass each other with the shared goal of making the individual feel loved and supported. Those relationships are among the most special in my life.

This book is a tribute to all of these wonderful people. If you worked with me at one time or another, and you wonder if the character of Maria, or Franklin, or Mona is based on you, the answer is yes; *yes, it is.*

ACKNOWLEDGEMENTS

Thanks to the people who I always sweep up in all my projects and who all manage to be gracious and sometimes enthusiastic, my family: Jeff, Kendall, Dan, Whitney, Chris, Ashley, Brett, Jenn, Robbie, Brendan, Adam, and Hudson.

A special thanks to Daniel Bader Designs for the cover, Anne Rowley for her knowledge of Communication and Debra Harkins for her editorial prowess and patience with a fledgling author.

Made in the USA
Middletown, DE
20 June 2021